Quiet Americans

Quiet Americans

STORIES BY

Erika Dreifus

Last Light Studio Books ~ Boston, Massachusetts

Published by Last Light Studio Books
423 Brookline Avenue #324
Boston, Massachusetts 02215

www.lastlightstudio.com

Book design by Joel Friedlander, www.TheBookDesigner.com

Printed in the United States of America

Publisher's Cataloging-in-Publication
     Dreifus, Erika.
          Quiet Americans : stories / by Erika Dreifus.
          p. cm.
          LCCN 2010930381
          ISBN-13: 9780982708422
          ISBN-10: 0982708424
          1. Short stories, American. 2. Jewish diaspora--
     Fiction. 3. Jews--Identity--Fiction. 4. Holocaust,
     Jewish (1939-1945)--Fiction. I. Title.
     PS3604.R45Q54 2011   813'.6
                    QBI10-600127

For my parents and JD,
and for R & S, and their namesakes

It doesn't end. Never will it end.
Günter Grass, *Crabwalk* (trans. Krishna Winston)

Which writer today is not a writer of the Holocaust?
Imre Kertész, Nobel lecture (trans. Ivan Sanders)

Contents

Acknowledgments

Many of the stories in this collection have appeared elsewhere (some in slightly different form): "For Services Rendered" in *Solander: The Magazine of the Historical Novel Society*, *J Journal: New Writing on Justice*, and on the *Scribblers on the Roof* website; "Matrilineal Descent" in *TriQuarterly*; "*Lebensraum*" in *Southern Indiana Review* and in the anthology *Becoming Fire: Spiritual Writing from Rising Generations;* "Homecomings" in *Jewish Education News* (as a first-prize winner of the David Dornstein Memorial Creative Writing Contest on Jewish Themes); "Floating" in *Mississippi Review Online*; and "The Quiet American, Or How to Be a Good Guest," in the anthology *Slower Traffic Keep Right*.

Residencies and scholarships from the Vermont Studio Center, the Kimmel Harding Nelson Center for the Arts, the Prague Summer Program, the Robert M. MacNamara Foundation, and the Paris Writers Workshop have supported and enriched this work.

I thank Last Light Studio Books and its publisher for their confidence and support.

Quiet Americans

For Services Rendered

His father and grandfather and great-grandfather had all practiced medicine in Berlin. Dr. Ernst Weldmann never questioned—rather, he embraced—the ancestral tide that swept him along a similar stream. Especially since his father's career had ended too soon, as so many others' had ended too soon, at Verdun.

But how could he explain the specific decision to treat the ills of the *young*? His wife, who had sought treatment in Vienna early in their marriage, espoused a theory that the motivation stemmed from his own childhood experiences. Of course, Klara knew about the death of his younger brother, then aged six, from scarlatina. And she had seen for herself the sadness in his sister, born less than a year after the burial. Almost from infancy Lise had seemed to recognize herself as the "replacement" child who could not quite compensate for the one her parents—and elder brother—had lost. Perhaps that was why she had married so young, escaped to her new husband's home, in Munich. She rarely wrote or visited. Sometimes, especially when he watched his own children playing, Ernst wished she would.

But most days Dr. Ernst Weldmann was far too busy for such reflections. The pace of his practice had, from the start, compelled him to employ an office manager, two nurses, and, each year, an intern selected from tens of applicants. In his desk he stored appreciative letters from those interns, and from parents of patients for whom he had cared in particularly acute circumstances.

On the walls he had placed his certificates and diplomas and the awards he had received from the municipal and even state medical societies. The bookshelves held not only his old textbooks but also the newer paediatric encyclopaedias to which he had contributed articles on scarlatina—the subject of a postgraduate fellowship, as Klara had reminded him. They contained, too, the neat volumes of *Deutsche Pädiatrie*, for which he had served as editor for six years. Until Jews could no longer occupy such offices.

He possessed a reputation, he knew, for being quiet and kindly, gentle and gentlemanly. The children seemed amenable to his ministrations; the mothers appeared to find in him a source of calm and comfort, even on the most alarming occasions.

"You never show how worried you may be," Klara said. "That helps."

In most instances Dr. Ernst Weldmann did not interact with his patients' fathers. Naturally *die Frauen* brought the children to his office. And when Dr. Weldmann visited their homes, only in extreme circumstances might the men be disturbed.

The situation was no different with the family of young Edda, whose mother was among the most attentive parents, despite her ceremonial obligations—as the Reichsmarschall's wife—and her more routine responsibilities running the family's favored residence at Karinhall. "The Second Lady of the Reich," the Reichschancellor had called her on the occasion of her marriage in 1935, because the Reichschancellor himself was unmarried.

As for Dr. Weldmann's own Lady, Klara worried and fretted, more and more. Of course, her distress was hardly new, dating back at least to the election in '33. But for a long time she'd said little in words; Dr. Weldmann could only read the dismay in the line of her mouth and the white of her knuckles when he could no longer treat insured patients, when the societies that had given him those awards dismissed him from their membership rolls, when two of his favorite professors, men who had arguably appeared most dedicated to the art and science of saving other people's lives, had ended their own.

But once he began treating the Reichsmarschall's daughter, Frau Weldmann spoke. Often.

"I don't understand it," she would say at the dinner table, while their twin daughters spooned soup or applesauce or custard into their mouths. "Surely he knows you're a Jew. And still he has you care for his daughter?" Klara had never seen the child, a flesh-and-blood being like any other; for her, Edda's name must conjure only images of the christening ceremony, chronicled by so many cameramen, pictures of the Bishop bestowing his blessing with the doting Reichschancellor in attendance.

Confronted with Klara's energy and conviction it seemed almost impossible for Dr. Weldmann to convey his own insights. In any case he wished she wouldn't raise the matter in front of Ruth and Rosa, who were barely old enough for kindergarten.

Perhaps he should not have told Klara about this case. Not revealed what had happened the summer day when the Frau Reichsmarschall—whom he'd recognized from the papers, naturally—had rushed into his consulting-room, a screaming toddler in her arms. A cinder had flown into the baby's eye while mother and child were strolling on the busy Ku'damm; the Frau Reichsmarschall had found a pharmacy at once. Was there a doctor nearby, the anxious Frau Reichsmarschall wanted to know? The sales clerk at the pharmacist's had recommended (surely with some hesitation, the doctor imagined) Dr. Weldmann, around the block. And that same day, impressed by his office, its journals and diplomas and most of all, she'd told him, his very self: the way he'd so smoothly managed to pacify the child and treat the eye within five minutes—and how Edda had squirmed and wriggled in her own mother's arms!—the Frau Reichsmarschall had insisted on having Dr. Ernst Weldmann serve as her daughter's paediatrician.

"Frau Reichsmarschall," he had said, quietly. Already the intern had stopped coming in, without even a word of farewell. And the office manager and non-Jewish nurse had explained that they could sustain the risks no longer. "I am quite willing to care for your child. But of course you realize that I am a Jew?"

The Frau Reichsmarschall had shrugged, then smiled at her little daughter. "What does that matter to me?"

But it mattered very much to Frau Weldmann.

"I don't like it." His wife shook her head, and set her soup spoon to rest. The twins, bless them, kept eating, while they exchanged glances from time to time. Occasionally one little girl whispered something to her sister. They still shared their own language at times; he had expected that habit to cease by this age.

"It frightens me," Klara continued. "That man frightens me."

He frightened many people, the Reichsmarschall. He seemed to accumulate jobs. Running the economy. Running the air force. He was a bulky man, who had been elected President of the Reichstag. He was said to be an inveterate hunter, which made him quite popular with the English. He opposed vivisection and was reported to keep a number of tamed animals, including a lion cub, as household pets.

This last piece of information Dr. Weldmann himself was able to confirm, when one evening in the early spring of 1939 he was summoned to Karinhall expressly to meet with the Reichsmarschall himself.

"What can he want with you?" Klara wondered, a bit of alarm beneath the bafflement.

The Reichsmarschall wasted no time.

"It would be advisable for you, Doctor," he began, his bulk behind his desk, his uniform still crisp and clean even late in the day.

Dr. Weldmann tried to stay focused. But he could not help wondering what other meetings the Reichsmarschall held in this room.

"In fact it would be most recommended," the Reichsmarschall was saying. "For you—to relocate. With your wife and children, of course."

Ernst Weldmann looked at the father whose two-year-old child his hands had touched, his clinical judgment had diagnosed, his prescriptions had cured. He recalled the siege—for it always felt as such, no matter how many times it was repeated or in which family, including his own—when one stubborn winter fever had stricken the little girl. These were older parents; it was a second marriage and the Frau Reichsmarschall had been forty-five years of age at Edda's birth. The child would likely be their only one.

He cleared his throat. "I am not certain that I understand you."

The other man opened a cigar box. "Please, Doctor."

"No, thank you." Dr. Weldmann suppressed the impulse to inquire whether cigars were also offered to the Reichschancellor during his visits. For the one element of the National Socialist program Ernst Weldmann admired was its anti-tobacco campaign. Of course, he would not have promoted it for the purpose of "racial purity."

"A drink, then?" The Reichsmarschall gestured to the liqueurs lining the top tray of an antique cart next to his desk. The place resembled a museum. Except for the lion cub—the doctor could scarcely believe the rumors were true but in fact it was a lion cub, and yes, this, too, the doctor could confirm, the Reichsmarschall did call the creature by a name. "Mucki" rested calmly among cushions in the corner.

The doctor declined the drink as well. This was not a social call.

The Reichsmarschall shrugged and selected a cigar. "I can say this no more plainly." He closed the box. "I would not wish to see you stay in Germany much longer. My wife, I know, would share this sentiment. In fact, it was Emmy who insisted—."

The doctor waited.

"She gets me into trouble," the Reichsmarschall confided, with a small smile. "Your case is hardly the first she has brought to my attention. My colleagues don't approve."

Dr. Weldmann recalled a conversation with the Frau Reichsmarschall, after the horrendous events of November. All of that had displeased her, she had told him. "And my husband was quite upset as well," she had said. "It was all quite contrary to Hermann's own policies, you understand, for the economic arena. 'A band of rowdies goes and destroys an enormous fortune in a single night,' he raved. Of course," she'd added, primly. "It would not be proper for me to discuss what he said about Jo—about his colleague who organized the—events."

Yes, Dr. Weldmann could see how the Frau Reichsmarschall might cause her husband a bit of trouble.

Klara Weldmann, too, could pose domestic difficulties. Her bluntness had alienated more than one of their neighbors. Her impatience with his mother had, until the elder Frau Weldmann's dying day, wounded the doctor; it haunted him still.

And so, that night after Ernst had returned from Karinhall and recounted all that had happened, he wasn't entirely surprised by her reaction.

"At least he's good for something," she said.

Ernst gave her a look, which he hoped she'd understand meant, *please lower your voice, as the children have only just gone to bed.*

"So let's go, then," Klara urged, her voice still strident. "If he's willing to help us."

She'd wanted to leave Germany for years, already. He was the one reluctant to abandon the land of his ancestors. He just refused to believe that this absurdity would continue. And had he not occupied something of a privileged position, son of a man fallen for the Kaiser? Remained exempt from so many of these decrees rather longer than his colleagues? But after November 9th—after nine of Berlin's twelve synagogues were torched and children from the Jewish orphanages made homeless and more than one thousand Jewish men sent away from the city—well, so much had changed.

"You know it will be impossible otherwise," Klara said. There, she had a point.

"But what about the rest of the family?" he asked. He'd last seen his sister when Lise had returned for their mother's funeral, with her lawyer husband and their young son. At the end of the burial he and Lise had stood together at the cemetery, apart from their spouses and children. He'd stared at his father's name, and then his brother's, on its own child-sized tombstone. He'd heard Lise take a breath, as if to speak. But then she had turned and walked away.

Perhaps he should ask if the Reichsmarschall might also arrange for Lise—.

"We must think about ourselves," Klara said, as if she had read his thoughts. "About the girls. We cannot risk having him become impatient." She paused. "I wouldn't even ask for my own family."

He struggled to look at her. As well as he knew her, he still could not believe that her eyes remained dry.

Frau Emmy Göring, on the other hand, restrained her tears only until Edda's governess had led the child from the room.

"I will miss you so very much," she said, clasping Dr. Weldmann's hands in hers. "Edda and I will miss you."

Ernst did not move, except to squeeze, cautiously, the Frau Reichsmarschall's hands.

"But it is the best thing for you," she continued. "For you and for your family."

His face felt frozen, yet Dr. Weldmann wished, wanted, yearned to say something. To thank her. And if he could do that, perhaps he could also manage to speak about his sister.

But just as a word seemed ready to slip from his throat and out his mouth, the Frau Reichsmarschall released his hands. She passed a handkerchief over her eyes and cheeks.

"I am glad that you are going," she said, her chin raised. "And glad that I could—."

And while he waited for her to complete the thought, she turned and left the room.

It was not that Dr. Ernst Weldmann's reputation preceded him to New York, precisely. But once he had established Klara and Ruth and Rosa and himself in a small apartment near the City College, with friendly downstairs neighbors; once he had located a few other émigré physicians and followed their instructions about commencing the process of practicing medicine in America; once he had fulfilled all the requirements and the referrals started streaming in, he needed, again, an office manager and a nurse and, ultimately, a young medical student to help manage all the children and all the mothers who sought his care and expertise.

Which was not to say that everything flowed smoothly.

For it seemed that his new country didn't quite welcome such an influx of immigrants, even skilled ones. There'd been new laws in New York, as well. In the end he had to wait five years for citizenship, while working rather humiliating jobs in hospitals (and serving as an intern, himself!). He'd been forced to supplement his income with lectures when he could (some, in New York, recalled his scholarship on scarlatina). And then he'd had to sit for another set of licensing examinations, of course. That he didn't mind. That he could have handled the first day they'd landed in New York.

But at least Ernst Weldmann and his family were in New York, not Berlin, when Germany attacked Poland in September 1939. They were in New York when Germany joined Japan in the war against the United States. They were in New York when those who had managed to survive the death camps (a group that Ernst soon learned, with a dull stab that was never quite to leave him for all the years that followed, did not include his sister, brother-in-law, or nephew) were at last liberated.

And they were in New York when the International Military Tribunal indicted the Reichsmarschall and his colleagues and commenced a trial in Nuremberg, in the fall of 1945.

One evening that fall, after the girls had cleared the supper table so they might settle there once more with their homework, Ernst retreated, as usual, to a chair in the living room. Klara brought him the newspaper. She glanced back quickly to the girls, then pointed to the front page's corner.

"Have you seen this yet?"

Sometimes he managed to read a bit before the evening meal, or between patients. But not that day.

Klara clasped her hands. "It's quite a lot to read." She sighed, then returned to the dishes waiting in the kitchen sink.

She was right. The entire Indictment appeared a few pages later. But Ernst somehow knew he needed to read only the last section in Count Four, beginning with the part on "PERSECUTION ON POLITICAL, RACIAL AND RELIGIOUS GROUNDS IN EXECUTION OF AND IN CONNECTION WITH THE COMMON PLAN MENTIONED IN COUNT ONE."

How clear and clipped it all seemed on the page: "These persecutions were directed against Jews. They were also directed against persons whose political beliefs or spiritual aspirations were deemed to be in conflict with the aims of the Nazis."

He kept reading: "Since 1 September 1939, the persecution of the Jews was redoubled: millions of Jews from Germany and from the occupied Western Countries were sent to the Eastern Countries for extermination."

The page blurred. *Sent to the Eastern Countries for extermination.*

"Papa, what's happened to Aunt Lise?" Rosa had asked, one horrible afternoon. He'd known it was only a matter of time, he'd known that at some point the twins would start asking questions he would not want to answer, would not be able to answer. If only he'd had this phrase at his fingertips that day, if only he'd been able to open his mouth and reply: "Your Aunt Lise? Ah, well—she was sent to the Eastern Countries for extermination." And if he'd found himself capable of saying that, perhaps he'd also have paused just another moment before continuing, perhaps even within Klara's hearing: "You see, your mother felt it would have been too much to ask someone—that we could not risk him becoming impatient with us."

He wiped his eyes and kept reading. Because after all that text, which seemed somehow preliminary information, came the profiles of each indicted man.

The doctor scanned until he found the paragraphs on Edda's father. How different, this postwar characterization of the Reichsmarschall. Really, he must stop thinking of the man that way! The war was over. Thank God. The Reich was no more.

The newspaper included a few photographs. How much weight the Reichsmarsch—he— had lost! But then, prison life could not be easy for the sybaritic king of Karinhall. Dr. Weldmann could not help wondering what had happened to little Edda, and to her mother. Where were they? How had they fared in the aftermath? He scoured the paper, but discovered little, save for the snippet about some families detained under guard.

Klara reappeared, wiping her hands on her apron. "They'll go after the wife, too, at some point," she sniffed.

He gave her a sharp look.

"What?" His wife's dark eyes flashed irritation. "It's the truth."

It wasn't the veracity of her comment that he questioned. And there was no doubt these men—Hermann Göring himself, and Rüdolf Hess and Martin Bormann and all the rest—deserved to be punished. Joseph Goebbels, the colleague whom Frau Emmy Göring had so delicately refrained from incriminating in her discussion of the events of November 1938, had committed suicide back in April, as had the Reichschancellor.

Still, no amount of punishment would bring back Lise, or her little boy or her husband, or Klara's relatives, or any of the millions who were now gone, forever.

Yet something had to be done.

But how much punishment? And who should decide? On what basis?

Klara's voice broke into his thoughts.

"I hope they rot," she said. "All of them."

"Klara," he warned, glancing over to the dining alcove and to the twins, still at the table.

Her eyes followed his. Her cheeks reddened.

"I need to iron the girls' dresses for tomorrow," she announced. And again she left him in his chair.

All of them.

He turned his eyes away from his daughters and thought of Edda. She would be seven—no, she would be eight now. Not much younger than another little girl had been—his sister—when their father was killed on a battlefield in France.

It was difficult to lose a parent so young.

He stared once more at the newspaper photographs. They were evil, these men. That's what Klara believed, that's what virtually everyone they knew believed. The neighbors downstairs, for instance, whom he and Klara had come to know fairly well; the two families now gathered for coffee and cake most Sunday afternoons. Those neighbors had lost both sets of parents, all siblings, countless nieces and nephews. At the hands of these evil men, even if only by their signatures. Surely, he must share the desire for retribution. Surely, having lost his only sister and her child, he must do more than understand it. He must agree.

But—should it make any difference if one of these men had effectively saved Ernst and Klara Weldmann and their two daughters? Did four lives matter, cast against the shadow of millions?

He held the newspaper closer, as if studying Hermann Göring's visage would provide an insight, an answer. He remembered the man's small smile emerging, and the phrase that had followed it.

Your case is hardly the first she has brought to my attention.

Should someone in authority perhaps be made aware?

He folded the paper, carefully. He did not need to decide just then.

"Are you crazy?" Klara asked a few evenings later, when, as they prepared for bed, he suggested that he might write to the Nuremberg tribunal. "Have you gone completely insane?" She studied him while gripping her hairbrush. "It's a serious question, Ernst. Did you inhale something at your office today? Accidentally inject yourself?" She patted his forehead with her free hand. "Or is there some new epidemic you haven't told me about?"

He pulled away. At that moment he simply did not want her touching him.

Why had he bothered to discuss this? Always, there had been so much about him she hadn't understood. Always, something about her heart had remained unyielding, beyond his comprehension.

But that was the point. So much remained beyond his comprehension.

"Everything is not always so black and white, you know!" The vigor in his voice stunned him, probably at least as much as it astonished Klara. Her eyes widened and she nearly dropped her hairbrush. For once, she seemed speechless.

"'All of them'!" He shook his head. "Everything is not always so clear!"

Klara watched him until he had pulled back the bed-clothes, hurled himself onto the mattress, and covered himself again. He closed his eyes but he could sense her watching him, still, for a long moment before she retrieved the hairbrush and resumed preparing for bed.

Late the next Sunday afternoon he and the girls had just returned from coffee and cake downstairs; Klara had remained to gossip still more.

"Papa, what are crimes against humanity?" Rosa asked.

His throat nearly closed. He sensed Ruth watching him.

"Where did you hear that phrase?" he managed.

Downstairs, it seemed. He must have been involved in another conversation. Perhaps it had even been Klara who mentioned the term, in the kitchen, with the women.

Both girls waited. A look of puzzlement spread across Rosa's face, an expression that was all that distinguished her from her twin, who studied him for a thorough moment and then supplied, "Maybe there's something about it in the newspaper."

"That's a good idea," he said, his voice nearly breaking. He didn't really want them reading about these horrors, either. But just then anything seemed preferable to discussing all of this directly.

His cowardice shamed him. "Look in the newspaper, then," he said, and settled in his chair in the living room, watching as his eleven-year-old daughters bent over the table, reading all about murder, extermination, enslavement, deportation, "and other inhumane acts…."

An image returned to his mind, a picture of that lion cub, curled against its cushions in Karinhall, and he heard the Reichsmarschall—Edda's father—offering him first a cigar, and then a drink from the antique cart, before making the very polite suggestion that Dr. Weldmann relocate. With his wife and children, of course.

"Although naturally Emmy and I will be sorry to lose you," the other man had concluded that night. "Emmy swears we won't be able to find anyone she'll trust quite so much with Edda."

Who was caring for Edda, now? And who would care for her, should she lose both parents? Unlike his own children, she did not even have a sister.

Lise. Lise. He pictured her that last day, at the cemetery, with her little son, and her husband.

Her lawyer husband.

The Reichsmarschall and his family could certainly use a good lawyer right now.

When was it, Dr. Ernst Weldmann tried to recall— and this question would return in irregular dreams and in unforeseen waking hours, on Holocaust Remembrance Days and on all those anniversaries of what would have been his younger sister's birthdays—that he had decided to specialize in the treatment of children, anyway?

At the table the twins still read. He could not leave his chair.

They'll go after the wife, too.

It was true. Frau Göring wouldn't be tried at Nuremberg, of course. But it would happen somewhere. Maybe he couldn't, in good conscience, write a letter defending the husband. The trial would reveal all Göring's misdeeds, and if there really were some other explanation or interpretation for his own expressed wishes to expunge Jews from the "economic arena," if he really hadn't known about the even more horrific measures his "colleagues" had taken—well, the truth would prevail.

But did that mean Ernst should—or must—remain silent about everything else? About her? About their last meeting, the clasped hands, the handkerchief? About, above all else, her happiness—yes, she'd been *glad*—that she had been able to help him?

He shifted in the chair, watched his daughters for a few more moments, then breathed deeply.

"Can one of you bring your father a pen?"

He said nothing further on the matter to Klara. He followed the news reports, which did, from time to time, mention Frau Göring and her daughter. So he knew that Frau Göring had been heard to remark, after seeing her husband for what may have been the last time, "that she realized that had the Germans won the war they would not have shown enemy leaders such considerations." He knew she'd been quoted as saying that "We have had our good days. We should not be surprised now to have bad ones."

"Very nice," Klara sniffed, after reading the same account. "But of course, even her worst day is nothing like what—."

He wanted to interrupt her. *Genug*, he wanted to say. Enough.

But he couldn't say anything. So he simply left the room.

Klara had been right: Frau Emmy Göring was, indeed, brought to trial, charged with "profiteering" from her Nazi connections. The *New York Times* reporter called her appearance in a packed courtroom at Garmisch "the greatest performance of her career," reminding everyone of the actress she'd been before she'd married the Reichsmarschall. Her health was in decline, the reporter said. She sat wrapped in blankets in the steaming courtroom. She wept. She gasped as she recounted the days, at the end, when Hitler had turned on her husband and ordered the death of the entire Göring family. Dr. Weldmann read that report and the ones that followed and so he knew, he read, he understood what had happened to her.

And yet he was still astonished—stunned—when the acknowledgment arrived. When he thought about it later he realized that it had arrived, in fact, almost exactly ten years after he'd been summoned to Karinhall to meet with the then-Reichsmarschall.

The letter came to his office. He waited until all the day's patients had been seen, all the staff had departed, and then he settled behind his desk and removed the opener from its place in the drawer that held, here in New York as it had in the corresponding furniture in Berlin, the old letters from former interns and grateful parents.

My dear Dr. Weldmann, the letter began. *I do not know how much of my story your American papers have continued to report. I am well, or reasonably so. The most important thing, of course, is that after a long separation I am once again with Edda. For that I believe it can be argued that I have you—and so many others—to thank.*

I was, I confess, very surprised and utterly moved by the many statements made in my behalf at my trial in Garmisch. Among these your letter, and other testimonies from Jewish circles, have meant the most to me. So unexpected, and so very much appreciated.

Dr. Weldmann set the letter down. A slight queasiness bubbled within him. This woman's husband had been sentenced to death at Nuremberg and avoided the punishment by killing himself. Now Frau Emmy Göring had survived the denazification and was living an apparently quiet life with her daughter. But where? Where could they live an ordinary life, in Germany? Had they returned to Berlin?

He inspected the envelope's postmark.

MÜNCHEN.

His heartbeat raced. His head pounded. Before him he saw not the letter on his desk, not the envelope with its postmark, but that final image of his sister, in the dark traveling suit that had served as a mourning outfit, too. She had come so far. But at the cemetery, when she might have said something he could now recall—even if they had been hurtful words—he'd attended instead to the already-dead.

Of course it isn't easy, Frau Göring continued in her

letter. *You may have heard that I was sentenced to a year in a labor camp, but in consideration of the time already served in detention, the judge released me.*

Still, a large amount of my property has been confiscated and I cannot return to the stage for five years. And with my conviction and sentence there remains a mark against my name, which I still hope to remove.

But she was alive.

And she was free.

And she was with her child.

He stuffed the letter back into its envelope. He didn't need to read the rest. Whether he'd show the letter to Klara one day; whether he'd destroy it; whether he'd leave it for one of his daughters to find that unnamed moment in the future when the girls would be left with all that remained—that was a decision for another time. For now, his job was done.

Matrilineal Descent

Weave back through the decades. Back before the *gästarbeiten*, before East and West Berlin, before the Wall; back before the Bunker, before the Führer, before Weimar. Keep weaving back, back, back; back before the railway car at Compiègne and before the Archduke was shot at Sarajevo, and you will find yourself in the time when the Kaiser still headed his empire. Then situate yourself more solidly in a small village of seven hundred souls, deep in a valley dotting the edge of the Black Forest. Altheim. And remind yourself that no one knew, then, about Zoloft.

It was too early even for electroconvulsive therapy, and unless you were Princess Marie Bonaparte or someone else of a life station considerably higher than that into which the object of our concern, Karoline Freiburg, was born, the term "psycho-analysis" meant nothing to you. (I can anticipate your comment, dear reader, as you observe that in France the physician Louis Victor

Marcé had long since published his *Traité de la folie des femmes enceintes, des nouvelles accouchées et des nourrices*. You would be correct, of course. But I would counter that for the Altheim midwives, the doctors and hospitals of Stuttgart and Heidelberg posed enough of a distant mystery; Docteur Marcé's comprehensive discussion and all those case studies might just as well never have been recorded or printed.)

And so (I would resume), when this woman, Karoline Freiburg, stopped eating and sleeping after the birth of her son; when for weeks and weeks those who passed by the bedroom window left open in that warm late springtime heard her weeping mingled with the baby's cries; when she confessed to her bewildered husband that at some moments (yes! it was true!) she considered throwing the child into the nearby stream; when she confided in her spinster sister that she didn't deserve to be a mother and that if something should befall her she wished that, well, Emma should take charge of raising little Josef, no one, not a single person in the village of Altheim—Catholic, Lutheran, or Jew—knew how to proceed.

Certainly it was not a matter of the villagers' indifference. In fact, Karoline was beloved to many. Her parents, distant cousins who shared the name of Gross (no sin to marry one's cousin back then) had themselves been born in Altheim, as had their parents, and theirs.

The records of the *Judengemeinde von Altheim*—records that traced the Gross family's presence in the village back to the expulsion of the Jews from nearby Etten-burg early in the eighteenth century, records that would survive the deportation of the village's Jews in 1940—noted that Solomon and Elisabeth Gross had welcomed Karoline, the youngest of their four children, on the twelfth day of May, 1888. That Karoline had married Jacob Freiburg, by trade a baker like his father-in-law, twenty-three years later. That Karoline gave birth twice. To a stillborn daughter. And to her son. Josef.

The records also show that Karoline Freiburg herself passed on 15 July 1914.

Those records reveal so much. Or so it would seem.

But this story, dear reader—this story is about what they do not tell.

The eldest of Solomon and Elisabeth Gross's four children, and the only other daughter, was Emma. Eight years Karoline's elder, Emma scarcely appreciated the addition of another female to the household in 1888, especially one so clearly her superior in feminine beauty even from the first day of life, an infant whose clear blue eyes compelled compliments from all the family's friends and neighbors, whose skin remained white and baby-soft even beyond babyhood, whose beaming made the rabbi's wife declare, when the child was just a few months old: "When Karoline Gross smiles, the sun shines all over God's good earth."

If Emma had not been what one would term a happy child before her sister's arrival, a definite gloom settled upon her then. A later analysis, of course, might have attributed this unfortunate development to the changes in her mother's availability, in the time and attention now dedicated to the newcomer, who seemed to strain Elisabeth's capacities in ways the two boys who preceded her had not.

"You already know how to manage that stitch, Emma," Mother now admonished. "You don't need me to show you again. Can't you see I'm busy with Karoline?"

And variations on that theme.

"Emma, be a little lady and help Papa in the bakery now, please, because Mother can't while she's taking care of Karoline, and the boys are too small."

"I'm sorry, Emma, but I really must rest now. You'll understand one day, when you're a mother, too."

But the more Mother made such comments, especially those remarks predicting Emma's domestic future, the more the little girl raged. Is it any wonder? Even then Emma knew the village women whispered about her. She knew people believed her to be plain, with her dull hair and eyes, her large hands and feet and features, her big teeth. She knew plain girls didn't easily find husbands, even in their village where muscles meant much more, in the end, than a pretty face. And she knew, almost from the day Karoline was born, that her younger sister would never have a problem finding a husband.

And her mother's defection was made all the worse by the disloyalty of her two brothers. Leo and Alfred seemed to delight in their littlest sister, whereas up to Karoline's arrival they had been Emma's charges, hers to lead and dominate. She had expected them to scream and yell about the newcomer, perhaps even to injure her in some small way. Indeed, for a time she even contemplated a plan by which one of the boys might—accidentally—tip the baby's cradle at some highly inappropriate moment.

But instead her brothers stood proudly by that impossibly sturdy cradle when anyone came to admire Karoline.

"Baby. Mine," three-year-old Alfred would say, pointing to himself, and making the visitors, and Papa and Mother, laugh.

Standing several feet away, Emma wouldn't laugh.

"So serious, that Emma!" the villagers said, shaking their heads, as they clustered outside the house after their visits.

Some sensed, and said, much more.

"Did you see, the scowl on that face?"

(One admittedly pessimistic and yet perceptive observer said: "If I were the mother, I'd be careful about leaving that girl alone with the little one.")

"As if the weight of the world rested on her shoulders."

What Emma never said, but felt within her heart and soul even from that eight-year-old time, was that in this baby that had arrived on the 12th day of May, 1888, the weight of the world had, indeed, fallen on Emma's own shoulders.

Karoline's was a much lighter spirit. As if the baby smiles had not indicated so much to the family, to the rabbi's wife, and to the rest of the village, the child's behavior bore out their early beliefs. Where Emma trod, heavy and clumsy in her boots, Karoline seemed to skim across the ground. Where Emma avoided the glances of others, Karoline's eyes shone full into those of her observers. Where Emma was understood to sigh, Karoline was known to sing. Such were their childhood constants.

And it was Karoline's lightness, her laughter, her spirit, that first attracted Jacob Freiburg when he arrived from Richen, a day's travel to the east, to acquire his master's license in Solomon Gross's bakery.

He arrived, this young man just a few weeks past

his twenty-second birthday (not that he had parents or siblings to mark it), at the family's doorstep. Richen offered him nothing; he had a trade, that was all, and when the news trickled to his town from Altheim that Solomon Gross sought an advanced apprentice, it did not take him long to pack his few clothes and leave.

"You'll come to us for supper," Solomon Gross said to the nervous young man that first day. "Emma, go tell Mother to set another place."

Jacob Freiburg appreciated the invitation, though he'd never, for the rest of his days, recall what was served. All he'd remember was that it was on that evening that he'd first met Karoline.

Apparently she'd worked in the bakery, too, but with his arrival she would now be free to help her mother in the home all the day. They handled some embroidery and weaving, Frau Gross explained, conversing before that first meal.

Karoline, said her mother, in a voice he'd had to lean rather uncomfortably close to the matron to hear, possessed considerable skills in these areas. He withstood the woman's sickly sour breath and was rewarded when Frau Gross showed him some of Karoline's handiwork. He had nodded, to demonstrate how impressed he was, while he fingered the fabrics ("You may touch them," Frau Gross had allowed). He'd glanced over at Karoline, first, and for a moment studied her hands, her skin, her long white fingers, realizing instantly that they were far better suited to needlework than to the pounding and kneading and scrubbing required at the bakery.

"And she isn't married yet, this Karoline Gross?" he asked, as discreetly and as soon as he could at a tavern later that week. He would spend a number of evenings in this tavern before his marriage, nearly any evening he was not invited to pass with his employer's family.

"The mother is ill, you know," one new friend confided. Then the man lowered his voice. "Some say she won't last long at all."

"I didn't know," Jacob said, then remembered her breath, and he resolved to be even more sensitive. His own parents were already gone, for years now; his had not been an easy youth by any standards, those of his own time or of ours, but it was not in his nature to reflect on his own troubles and deprivations. How much more difficult this prospective loss must be, he thought, for so feminine a creature as Karoline. How she must be suffering, in this time when her mother was so weakened by illness. An angel, she must be, an angel of comfort helping her mother in the home now.

"Have some bread," one of the other men said, pushing a plate toward Jacob. "You need to be fattened up."

The embarrassment! But it was true. In the past year or so, despite what seemed to be constant eating and drinking, his clothes had fitted ever more loosely. But that wasn't worth thinking about right now. He'd simply eat more, drink more to slake what seemed a constant thirst.

Jacob learned from his new neighbors, too, that it wasn't that unusual in Altheim for marriages to be delayed. For children to stay at home a little longer, to help their parents with family businesses. Karoline, he knew, was already twenty-one.

"They'll have that Emma for quite awhile, that's for sure," another man remarked. Two or three others guffawed and beer spilled from their mouths into their beards.

Jacob laughed, too (it was important to be polite). But he didn't find Emma as unlikable as others seemed to. In some respects he even admired her. She was brisk, efficient. He'd already seen that she knew how to accomplish things in the bakery. She'd been there, working, by the time he'd arrived each of these past few days. But she had barely spoken to him.

He pitied her. He imagined it must be very difficult to be Karoline's sister, to sit in the shadow of such brightness and beauty. But he could scarcely focus on pitying Emma when he was consumed with the worry that another man might win Karoline over before he could accomplish that feat! His eyes narrowed. He reexamined his companions at the table. Which of them might be his competitors? Which might be secretly trying to make Karoline his wife, right now?

"And the boys are no use," said another man, a fat specimen with pimples to one side of his nose, which he'd just wiped on his sleeve. "One does nothing but study." (This, Jacob understood, was Leo, whose absence Frau Gross had explained away: "The rabbi sent him to the city!"). And then there was Alfred, whom Jacob had in fact met. What could one say of Alfred, kindly? The gentlest thing, perhaps, was that he was somewhat dim, and that his mother always talked of the lovable child he was and continued to be.

At work Jacob tried to learn the business of this bakery as quickly as he could. For if Solomon Gross decided that he had become indispensable—like a son, perhaps, a son that might succeed him—well, surely that could only help his cause.

In this enterprise Jacob believed he could enlist some assistance, for he sensed that Emma did not find him entirely unsympathetic. At times he caught her staring at him. Once or twice he even thought he saw her smile.

"Tell me, Emma," he said, drawing near to her as she prepared the Sabbath breads, once he felt they had spent enough time together for the familiarity. "Tell me how you go about this challah…." He'd ask for her advice, her instructions, even if he did not really need them. Of course he already knew how to bake a challah! But surely it wouldn't hurt to win the sister over, as well. Especially if—when—the mother …. Emma, he could see, would take over that role of matriarch. He expected, and hoped, to be part of her family for a long time to come.

You might imagine, the effect on Emma. For no man had ever spoken to her with such deference and respect. No one cared to hear what she might say. No man—except Jacob Freiburg.

It was almost too much to hope for. She'd tried to ignore the almost instant stirrings that had disquieted her from the day he'd arrived, the first moment he'd knocked on their door and asked if this was the home of Solomon Gross. She'd tried.

She dreamed that one day they might run the bakery together, alone. He was serious and well-meaning. She liked his warm brown eyes. She imagined resting her head on his shoulder. She watched him kneading the bread and stared at his hands, his fingers.

Maybe they could do more than run the bakery together, she thought at night, when she lay alone under her heavy quilt, half-awake, listening for the moans from her mother's sickbed.

For his part, Jacob never quite understood why

Emma, who seemed to have warmed to him just slightly more as they continued to work in the bakery, retreated into stone silence again after the engagement was announced.

"Your sister—is she well?" he asked Karoline, the afternoon they took their first unchaperoned walk along the forest's edge.

"Why do you ask?"

He explained. Karoline listened. Her face seemed to change; she asked a question, then another; the light faded from her brilliant eyes but then, in a blink or two, it returned.

"Oh, that's just Emma," Karoline assured him, smiling. "She's so serious."

"Do you think that's all?" he asked, daring to squeeze her hand and lift it to his lips. The idea that all of her, every limb, every inch of skin, every curve, would soon be his to touch and see and smell and kiss was almost too much to bear.

"Let's not talk about Emma," she answered, squeezing back.

Karoline, no longer Gross, loved that first year of marriage, which was marred only by the increasing weakness of her mother, and the corresponding sadness of her father. When she wasn't tending her mother (Emma took over as soon as she could leave the bakery each day), she spent most of her time caring for her own little home, just across the yard from her parents' house, a three-room cottage that was all theirs, hers and Jacob's, that was filled with light all day, and love almost every night.

So it was not long before Karoline could announce a first pregnancy. But perhaps it was already an ill-fated one. For it began shortly after a death, that of Elisabeth Gross, and ended in another one—that of Karoline's baby itself.

Karoline had sensed something was wrong, toward the end. The baby had stopped moving.

"Something is not right," she told Jacob. She even confided in Emma. Had she any choice, without Mother? It did make her uncomfortable, especially when she remembered what Jacob had said of Emma's odd behavior when the engagement was announced. Then there was the way her sister stared at her all throughout the pregnancy. But she felt sorry for Emma, too. Once, seeing Emma gaze at her from across the table she had actually offered, "Would you like to feel the baby, Emma? It's—active, right now?" And Emma had flushed scarlet, pressed her lips together, and fled the room.

But when she spoke about her fears, Emma was all coolness.

"Nonsense," her sister had said. "You're just nervous. It's normal. I imagine."

But then the labor, the pain, the blood, the pain, and for what? A dead baby, no cry, no movement, and they had insisted, the midwives, that Karoline look at the infant girl, look at her and do more than that. They had insisted that she hold her.

"It will be good for you," the midwives said.

But Karoline didn't want to look at the nonliving child she had produced, she didn't want to hold death in her arms, she didn't want to confront next to her breast her failure as a wife, as a mother, as a woman, right there and then. She just wanted to be alone, to sleep, and to cry.

"You'll be fine," the midwives said, bundling up the bloody linens. "In a few weeks you'll be good as new. You'll bury this one and you'll have another in a year."

They were almost correct. For her body healed, at least, and it wasn't too many months later that she conceived for the second time.

Dread dominated the second pregnancy. Karoline was certain that she could not produce a living child. What use was she? She might as well be dead herself. This she repeated every day, while she lay, pale and unwashed, in the wide bed where both children had been conceived.

"You should have married someone else," she told Jacob who stood in the doorway, gazing at her.

He seemed struck speechless.

"You should have married my sister," she said.

"Karoline!"

But the idea had seized her and it grew every day, developing along with the child inside her. Sometimes the thoughts burst from her head onto her tongue and into the air where her husband heard them. Emma knew how to be capable. Emma could produce. Look how well she had cared for their mother. Look how well she had taken over the bakery, now that Papa was so sad and silent he could barely shuffle to the baking table every day. (Loyal as she was, Karoline knew she could not credit Jacob with the business's survival.) And if Emma had delivered a stillborn child (God forbid!) you could be sure she wouldn't be sitting around all day, sighing and weeping and sleeping.

"Karoline, dearest," Jacob ventured one day. "Perhaps we might go for a walk? Just out behind the house? By the stream, perhaps?" He paused. "It would do you good—and the baby, too." Here he stared at her round belly, rising beneath the sheet. "To get some air?"

She said nothing.

Jacob paused, then an expression came over his face, as if he had discovered a pot of gold.

"Karoline, my love, I only suggested it because—I asked Emma first and—well, she thought it was a good idea."

Karoline turned in the bed, to avoid her husband's stare. After what must have been several long minutes, she pulled herself upright.

"Find my shoes," she said.

This baby survived the birth, but his mother nearly did not. So weak was she that she could not nurse him for the first week; she could not venture from her bed to sit, comforted by the other women, while the men attended his ritual circumcision; for nearly three weeks she could not even hold him without the support of a pillow and her sister's close and watchful eye. And then, when others expected her to shower him with the love she might have given his elder sister, she waited for others to lift him, crying, from his cradle and bring him to her breast.

"What kind of mother am I?" she wondered, aloud, while Emma placed the crying baby back in the cradle Karoline herself had once occupied, the cradle Emma had once studied while complicated thoughts boiled within her head.

Staring at the baby, Emma said only: "He looks exactly like his father."

No reassurances from Karoline's husband sufficed. No declarations of love and gratitude for the remarkable gift she had given him—a son to name for his own departed father!—no protestations that in motherhood she was even more beautiful than she had been as a maiden could convince her of her value in Jacob's eyes.

"Look at me," she said. "Look how pale. Look—." She pointed to this mark, to that fold, to anything that could possibly be construed as a blemish.

And because the midwives had warned him not to touch her yet, Jacob could not prove how wrong she was.

It was Emma who found her, and told him in words he quickly translated.

"She did away with herself," Emma said.

"She died some way—." Such was how he chose to hear it, and how it remained in his memory. "She died some way—." And then he thought further, he thought of what "some way" could have been, for even in that shocking moment he knew that there must be an explanation to give the child, one day, where his mother had gone, why she was not right there, in the home. An illness. An accident. A fire, even. He did not ever tell his son the truth, he could not bring himself to accept the reality that spread quickly through the village, he did not stop to think that one day other voices might recount this reality to his son, even if his did not.

But how can we blame him? For how could this man accept (let alone envision telling his son) that Karoline Freiburg had risen from her bed, left her son alone to be discovered screaming and soiled in his cradle, and wandered—shoeless—to the stream just yards away from her home, where she drowned herself?

Jacob had little time to linger in his own private grief. For with the assassination of an Austrian Archduke that summer of 1914, the Angel of Death's fingers began to reach far beyond his own family.

"I have to go," he said, placing a letter on a dry, clean corner of the kitchen work table. He moved to the sink, filled a glass with water, drank it within seconds, and refilled the glass.

Emma wiped her hands clean from the flour. She seated herself and unfolded the letter.

"I'm sorry," he said, before she'd finished reading. "I don't want to leave." He sensed himself weaken, become almost faint. What kind of soldier was he going to be, anyway? What kind of Imperial Army would make use of him?

"Yes," she said.

"I don't want to leave you," he said, reaching for the edge of the stove to steady himself, hoping he would not burn his hand.

She glanced up, said nothing.

He gestured to the table with its rolling pins and bowls. "I don't want to leave you with the bakery."

"Ah, yes. With the bakery." Then her glance seemed

to sharpen into a stare. "And, I expect, with Josef?"

His face warmed. "Well, ah, yes. Of course. I mean—who else would—but, Josef—I mean, he is hardly a burden? Surely you don't regret caring for him?"

She said nothing.

He kept speaking. "Because, of course, you love Josef. He is of Karoline. How can you not?"

She folded the letter. "We'd best begin preparing."

He nodded. But he could not think of any preparations just then. Just then he needed, more than anything else, another glass of water.

If, when Jacob left the house late that summer, he had turned back—if he had run home to hold his infant boy one last time, if he had decided he must reassure himself that his child was going to be well cared for—he would have found Josef still screaming, alone, for hours, screaming until there was no sound left to emerge from his poor raw throat, while Emma went about her business, cleaning and cooking and thinking that a child so ill-behaved did not deserve to be fed that day. Discipline. That was what a child needed.

That was what her sister had lacked.

The child was so hungry that as soon as he could walk he toddled in front of the house, frailly, and he ate stones from the yard.

This memory Josef Freiburg would not retain, of course. But the villagers saw it happen. They saw. Catholic, Lutheran, and Jew. They saw the motherless little boy, whose father had been compelled to leave him, whose father might never return. The little boy who possessed the potential for so much brightness but who could not bloom at all, in that house.

"She's an evil woman, that Emma Gross," more than one of them repeated.

"There's always been something unnatural about her."

"You could see it in her as a child, already. Remember, when the younger sister—may she rest in peace—was born? Remember Emma, back then?"

Some said more. Why hadn't Emma tended to her sister the way she had cared for her mother? Why hadn't she seen to it that Karoline obtained some fresh air, once in awhile? Early morning or evening walks, for example? Accompanied, of course. You didn't let a woman like that wander along by herself. And why hadn't Emma kept her sister cleaner, better fed, more appropriately attired? Was it really so difficult to imagine how much more melancholic Karoline must have felt—for after a time the villagers seemed to acquire a surprising degree of clinical awareness that had eluded them throughout Karoline's illness—left in her dark bedroom, in the bed that was never made, the air heavier and more oppressive as the summer wore on?

"I worry," said the rabbi's wife, recalling the smile of the infant Karoline and thinking of her son. "I worry about the child."

And so one day the rabbi went to see Solomon Gross. He told Solomon that he understood how much had changed in the household, since the tragedies. Still, there was a child to be taken care of.

"There should not be another tragedy," the rabbi said, and watched as old Solomon's eyes filled and overflowed.

Thus began the child's career in the bakery.

Now move ahead, after the war, after the peace. Jacob returns. He must find a wife.

You might wonder if he chose Emma? But of course not. He was never truly interested in Emma and by then someone else had grown into womanhood nicely enough to catch his attention.

Besides, the villagers didn't let Emma's misdeeds go unreported.

He had another child with the new wife. Another son. And they certainly did not live happily ever after.

Recall, if you will, the allusion to 1940 back at the beginning of this story.

Jacob didn't even survive that long. That thirst wasn't so insignificant, for he was a diabetic, before insulin became widely available. He might have had a better chance in Canada, or the United States, that early. But medical care in Altheim, as you may have surmised, was hardly the best.

Solomon died of old age before the *Kristallnacht*. And Jacob's second wife died of complications in childbirth. Her child lived but a few months without her.

Josef—well, that's another story. He grew up. And he got out. He was in America in 1937.

Now, some people ask—and perhaps you may be among them—"What happened to Emma?"

Keep looking ahead. Go, now, after all these decades and even after the turn of another century, to the district clerk's office, or to one of the libraries where you will find the published volume holding the records of the *Judengemeinde von Altheim*. Turn enough pages and eventually you will read of Emma Gross: *für tot erklärt seit 30 Oktober 1940*.

And if you don't read German, I'll translate.

"Believed dead"—since the day she was deported.

Lebensraum

I t was May of 1944, when the orders came to the men at Fort Sheridan, Illinois. In days, they would leave to make ready a prisoner-of-war camp, in a town called Clarinda.

Another soldier working in the officers' mess with Josef Freiburg nodded. "I know the place. Iowa. About eighty miles southeast of Omaha."

But that information hardly helped Josef.

After the bus and the train and the other bus how empty this Camp Clarinda seemed. How much quiet. How much land. Josef stood close to his duffel. In the distance he could see the barracks, and watchtowers. The barbed wire, of course, he could nearly touch. But there were trees, too, and grass that seemed to reach so very far.

He didn't want to begin here without a moment for prayer. In the duffel he found the little brown book with the cloth cover, the *Readings from the Holy Scrip-*

tures for Jewish Soldiers and Sailors.

"Better watch out, Reverend," the others sometimes told the chaplain, with a wink. "Joe, here, wants your job." Always the chaplain smiled in response, and shook his head. At Passover he'd consulted Josef about *matzoh.*

"You're the baker, Freiburg," he'd said. "You know what to do." The chaplain, too, had made the trip from Fort Sheridan.

Josef squinted, under the sun, to read again the letter on the brown book's first page, from Mr. President Franklin Delano Roosevelt.

To the Members of the Army:

As Commander-in-Chief I take pleasure in commending the reading of the Bible to all who serve in the armed forces of the United States. Throughout the centuries men of many faiths and diverse origins have found in the Sacred Book words of wisdom, counsel and inspiration. It is a fountain of strength and now, as always, an aid in attaining the highest aspirations of the human soul.

For Josef this was all such beautiful, high language. Yet it was the freedom in the words that mattered. Back in Germany such a book would have been burned away.

He turned the page. "Presented to Private First Class Josef Freiburg."

On the next line: "Home address: 200 Pinehurst Avenue, New York, New York."

And then: "Nearest of kin: Nelly Freiburg (wife)."

The moments with the book ended when a voice sounded through a megaphone. Josef glanced up to see a tall, red-haired man shouting. "I am Lieutenant Donaldson. And before even welcoming you to Camp Clarinda, I have the privilege of reporting the victory that has taken place in Normandy. President Roosevelt will address the nation this evening." Cheers and applause followed.

Josef remembered Normandy, and the outline of Cherbourg as the ship sailed away. He'd had one day in Paris, too, where the train from Stuttgart had left him. That city had frightened him, almost, so busy and so beautiful. It all seemed so long ago, the story of his departure. An uncle he'd hardly known, an uncle named Leo, a professor in Heidelberg, had summoned him to that city, told him what he knew and how he knew it, told him that Josef had to get out, told him that he, Leo, owed his dead sister, the mother Josef had never known, that much. That he owed it to Josef, too.

But now Josef must receive his assignment.

At Fort Sheridan, it was food service, preparing breads and pastries for the officers. Sometimes guilt filled him, for should he not be sacrificing more for his new country? How difficult was it, for him, to rise before dawn? This he had done even in advance of the time Father died, a year before they discovered the insulin.

The lieutenant checked his clipboard. "I see congratulations are in order, Soldier."

Josef opened his mouth, then closed it. Did the lieutenant know about the baby to come to him and Nelly in the fall?

"Your naturalization," the lieutenant said. "All official, now."

All official. But what was it Nelly had said about that? "A long road to travel."

How his Nelly talks. When the call came for the draft, she said: "They're not sending you anywhere without citizenship." Then she looked at his big black shoes that always cost so much. "Although with your feet, they won't send you very far. You would hold the whole company back." She laughed.

But the citizenship was not so funny. There were many forms, and money orders, and lists of the places where he lived after 1937, and worked. The Hanscom Bakery. The New York Pie Company. Nelly wrote the names and dates, in her pretty writing.

Other people wrote, too. Friends who were already citizens supported him. "I was naturalized in the Southern District of New York on the 21st of March 1937, and I assure you Josef Freiburg is of good character, and will make a good loyal United States citizen as I know he is happy to be in this great country." Another: "I have known Josef Freiburg since a year and a half. I find Mr. J. Freiburg to be honest and trustworthy. I was myself born in Karlsruhe, Germany, on December 2, 1911 and immigrated to the United States in October 1935...."

And he answered questions himself. He told how he supported the effort for war. How last year he bought four defense bonds, each for twenty-five dollars. He told how he was not "in possession" of ammunition, short-wave receiving sets, transmitting sets, signal devices. He was not even sure what meant all such things; he just kept shaking his head.

The lieutenant spoke again. "Well, soldier. You have a very important job here."

Josef stood as straight as possible.

"We have four kitchens at this camp. You will take charge of one."

A mistake, surely. "I beg pardon?"

"Yes, it's a big job." The lieutenant tucked the clipboard under his arm. "We're going to have three thousand prisoners here, eventually. But you'll have help."

"Help?"

Silence. "Some prisoners." More silence. "From Europe."

The lieutenant, he could not possibly mean—.

"Germans."

("Smart man. He was careful not to use the word 'Nazis,'"said Nelly, later.)

Then the lieutenant stepped closer and tapped Josef's arm. Josef almost jumped.

"Don't worry, Freiburg," he said.

Josef worried. And not only about those Nazis about to descend like a plague on Egypt. Crossing the ocean, first, as he had not too many years past. Then crossing the country, part of the way at least. Maybe they, too, would find it remarkable, the almost endless land of this America. A day could go by, and then another, and still one would not be at its other border, at the ocean on its other side.

But he worried not only about them. Because Nelly arrived. All the time he thought of her, and of the baby. Camp Clarinda's medical facilities could not meet the needs of a woman in Nelly's condition, but the town had a new municipal hospital, where babies were born.

In all his memories he could not find such joy as in the news of this baby. It would, of course, be a son. Handsome. With dark, curly hair and maybe Josef's own brown eyes. He would go to school. He would be a doctor, one day. Or a lawyer. Or a rabbi. Or maybe even President of the United States of America.

But not a baker. Never. Josef will cut off his boy's hands first. It is good and honest work. But his son—

his son will go to school. He will do more. Better.

Nelly was not so enthusiastic, and not only for the physical reasons he imagined all females feared.

"How are we going to feed a baby?" she demanded, when first she had told him the news. In moments such as these her blue-gray eyes always looked cloudy and made him think about the winter ice on the stream behind his house in Altheim. "We can't always feed ourselves."

True, back at home in New York. But in Clarinda, in the country's basket of bread—Josef liked that phrase and repeated it often—the corn crops alone promised food enough. Mrs. Johnson, their landlady, grew a vegetable garden and brought them fat red tomatoes fresh from the vines. Still Nelly worried, especially since in her family there had been many twins, and once she'd located a doctor in Clarinda she insisted that he arrange for an x-ray to make sure that she was carrying only one child, not two.

"If only you ate pork," she'd sigh in pretend-sadness when she prepared a favorite pea soup, which she'd told him as a child she'd always eaten prepared with bacon. "Then we could really feast, every night." Nelly came from a big city, after all. To her parents, the religion was never so important. But even without pork, it was good to watch Nelly's middle expand. Sometimes he could not believe he was husband to this fine lady who spoke such good English. Only here, in America, where they had both arrived as refugees, both lived in Yorkville, both found work (she as a governess in the home of a rich Jewish family), both happened to spend part of the same day off visiting the same friend, also a refugee, who was recovering from the pneumonia. Josef had admired her from that first meeting, and when they both took leave of the friend he had asked when he might see her again.

Sometimes Lieutenant Donaldson stopped by the kitchen. Josef usually had a slice of apple cake or a sweet roll set aside for him, or for the chaplain, who also visited from time to time. He was not certain why they seemed to have become his friends. Perhaps for Lieutenant Donaldson, it had something to do with what the man had said to Josef one day. He'd been raised to believe that the Jews were God's Chosen People, he said, but until he'd met Josef, he'd never even known a Jew, personally. Whatever the reasons, Josef was grateful. Especially when the chaplain or lieutenant might offer him a ride into town and he might be home a little earlier, to spend more time with Nelly. So far the work was not so heavy, since the prisoners had not yet arrived and Josef had only to worry about feeding the Americans.

On one of those trips from the camp into Clarinda,

Lieutenant Donaldson cleared his throat. "The men will be here on Friday, Freiburg. Friday morning. We're trying to keep it quiet. Don't know how the good people of Clarinda are going to react, really. A lot of them have their own boys over there." He paused. "Of course it will take time for these fellows to be processed. But you'll have your staff before the end of the day."

Josef's heartbeat quickened. Would he be done with them in time for the Sabbath? For his private prayers before Nelly returned from reading the Chicago papers at the public library?

"You should get them working right away," the lieutenant continued. "Saturday morning breakfast isn't too soon. Because of course they all have to eat, too."

"Yes, sir."

The lieutenant glanced away from the road for a moment. "They're mainly farm boys themselves. Not the political ones. They've been checked."

As Josef left the jeep the lieutenant cleared his throat again. "Don't worry, Freiburg."

After supper that night Josef stood. "Stay," he told Nelly. "I clear the table."

His hands shook and the plates crashed in the sink. He heard Nelly pull herself from the chair.

"What's wrong?" she asked.

He should never have told her.

"Friday."

Nelly's hands moved to her apron. "I see." A silent moment followed. Then: "They can't do anything to you, you know."

He knew. He wore the uniform of a soldier in the United States Army, and here in the big clean rooms on the second floor of Mrs. Johnson's house on Maple Street Nelly kept the naturalization certificates in a desk drawer, in a brown envelope along with the book from the bank and the defense bonds and their marriage license. But those men had chased him away before, because the Fatherland wasn't large enough for all of them to live. How would they fit together in the Camp Clarinda kitchen?

"Maybe I speak broken German?" He blinked very fast. "Maybe they think I am American trying to be nice?"

Nelly shook her head. "They'll know. But do as you like."

Friday afternoon he found in his kitchen three rows of ten prisoners apiece, with white faces and eyes that had red streaks. Even if he'd wanted to watch them arrive in town he wouldn't have been able to. He'd had the kitchen to tend.

He worried that he might be sick. "*Guten tag*," he began. He held a clipboard to keep the hands steady.

Did any eyes widen, at the German? He could not be sure. When he next spoke he chose English words.

"We begin at 4:30 each morning." He breathed once, then again. "These will be your jobs."

They were young, these boys. Some had to be at least ten years younger than Josef himself. They stood straight, yes, at attention. But those eyes were tired. And even, Josef thought with some disbelief, worried.

"Of course they're worried," Nelly said, later that evening. "A German doesn't expect such good treatment in prison."

Maybe she was right. The next morning the men seemed to walk around the kitchen for the first hour simply staring at all the food. The milk. The bread. The eggs. They murmured among themselves, but not so low that Josef couldn't understand them. Apparently they hadn't seen so much food in a long time, and not only because they'd been called to military service. Josef's chest tightened.

But then, just as the group seemed more at ease, each man at work at a particular task with Josef supervising a cluster at the hot oatmeal pots, he swore he heard it. The word.

"*Jude.*"

He spun around. The men all faced the stoves, or stared at sinks, holding pitchers beneath the faucets. Except for the one next to an open refrigerator. His face was red. His name was Weber.

What to do? Maybe the imagination was playing tricks. Even if Weber had said this word, what did it matter now, here? Was not Josef safe and free? Was not Weber the one imprisoned?

Josef stepped closer to Weber. "When you finish," he nodded at the carton of eggs in the other man's grasp. "Another job for you."

Weber said nothing.

An hour later Lieutenant Donaldson arrived. Josef saluted.

"Everything in order, Freiburg?" the lieutenant asked.

Josef's eyes met the lieutenant's. "Do not worry, sir."

And so it went, over the next weeks. No real problems. Some of them even hummed while they worked. Smiled at him. The older ones (older—his age!) talked about their own wives and children, after Lieutenant Donaldson mentioned Nelly and the baby during one of his visits.

"I bet they'll want to stay, afterward," Nelly said one night. "They have it pretty good, here."

She spoke some truth. Here, of course, food could be had and the clouds moved quietly in the sky. Everyone had clothing to wear and a place to sleep at night. Such was not the case back in Germany. And as for the work—it was hard, but a man should work hard.

"But why would they not go home?" he asked her. "Does not everyone want that, truly? To go home?"

She did not answer.

On Sundays Nelly liked for them to go walking. She spoke often of such times in the countryside with her father. But her footsteps grew heavy as her time approached.

They had just crossed the town lines one afternoon when they began, again, the discussion about the child's name. And then Josef cleared his throat.

"*Liebchen.*"

Leaves crunched beneath their feet.

"Maybe we should try to find a *mohel* after all."

Nelly breathed faster.

"I mean, this will be our first son, and after everything—." Why could he not explain, not in his native language, not in his adopted one, the feelings? After this time supervising Nazis ("They aren't all necessarily Nazis, Freiburg," Lieutenant Donaldson had repeated, several times. "Please try to remember that."). Giving them knives—to slice bread. After months listening while Nelly reported from the newspapers she read at the library. About what was not yet over, in Europe. Watching Nelly write letter after letter to her mother in South America; the United States had not welcomed Josef's mother-in-law, not yet anyway, but Nelly's brother had lived in Brazil since 1931 and had managed to get their mother a visa. For the day and night after she mailed or received each letter, Nelly would become very, very quiet.

And the dream, his own dream, his own sadness: his grandfather, wrapped in the prayer shawl Josef managed to carry on the ship. Wrapped in the shawl and chanting the prayers and blessings that Josef still recited every day, every Sabbath, every festival, even if he hadn't entered a house of worship since 1937, since he was last in Altheim, since he last stood at Opa's still-fresh grave. If his grandfather had lived, Josef might not have left, no matter how much his uncle in the city had tried to persuade him.

Josef could not think more of that grave, of the graves of his father, or of the graves of his two mothers and his stillborn siblings, or of the old synagogue that maybe did not survive the *Kristallnacht*. He knew, only, that he wanted for the baby the ritual circumcision. The *bris*.

But Nelly seemed unwilling to talk. "What if 'he' is a 'she'?" she challenged. And it was a good question.

So they spoke no more on this question. Until the baby was born.

"I have important message for Brazil," Josef told the

man at Western Union that day, and then he took from a pocket on his uniform the address for Nelly's mother, on the paper Nelly had given him with the message printed, too.

EIGHT POUNDS TWO OUNCES MICHAEL JACOB NELLY FINE STOP.

"Congratulations," said the man. "Tell you what. I'm not even going to charge you. You're assigned over at the camp, right?"

Josef nodded. "But I must pay!"

"No," the man insisted. "You buy something for your wife, instead."

He brought her flowers. And he waited one whole day after Michael Jacob's birth to try to reason with her about the *bris*.

"We're in a community completely without Jews, Josef." She sat against her pillows, holding the folded newspaper the librarian had brought her. Other ladies dozed, read magazines, talked softly with their husbands. "Our family and friends are so far away. The most sensible thing is for the hospital to handle it."

How to answer that? In the silence, Josef heard boot-steps approach. He looked over to see two familiar faces nearing Nelly's bed.

Both visitors smiled. "Well, well, Mrs. Freiburg. You're obviously feeling good and strong," said the chaplain. Lieutenant Donaldson stood beside him.

"Congratulations, Freiburg." The lieutenant extended his hand. "You've got a fine-looking little fella in that nursery."

A wave of joy swept through Josef. Until the chaplain spoke.

"And what, may I ask, are the plans for the circumcision?"

Josef studied the floor. "The hospital. The hospital will take care."

"The hospital?" The chaplain frowned. "I'm sorry, but this child deserves a *bris*, and that's all there is to it."

Nelly said, "And how, Reverend, do you propose to get a *mohel* here, or enough Jews for a *minyan*, or the money we'd need?"

The lieutenant bowed. "Ma'am, you just leave that to us."

And everything was in order by the baby's eighth day. Jewish men from Omaha volunteered to travel the 80 miles to witness the ceremony. One contacted the *mohel,* not so easy because, he explained, "the man covers North Dakota, South Dakota, Nebraska, and Iowa."

Changed from her robe and bed-gown to a dress for the first time since the birth, Nelly stood with Josef outside the operating room to greet the neighbors Mrs. Johnson had alerted, and the librarian, and the Army comrades who had been with Josef since Fort Sheridan.

"You are all right?" Josef asked his wife, as he adjusted his grandfather's prayer shawel around his shoulders. "You want to sit down?" He pointed to a chair a few feet away.

Nelly shook her head. Then she leaned against the wall. "Maybe you're right," she said. "Maybe I should sit."

Josef brought the chair over to her.

She lowered herself to the seat, slowly. At first he thought she might smile, relax a little bit.

But she did not. Her eyes looked like ice. "You know that most of these people are here out of curiosity more than anything else," she warned him. "It'll be a long time before Clarinda sees its next *bris*."

He thought about what she was saying. "But don't you think, *Liebchen*, that people might be happy for us? Good-will?"

Before she could answer the lieutenant approached. He greeted them both, then cleared his throat. "Freiburg, there's something I want to ask you," he said. "If we might speak for a moment?"

"I'll be fine," Nelly said.

Josef and Lieutenant Donaldson stepped around a corner.

"Freiburg—may I carry the baby into the room?" the lieutenant asked.

Josef was unsure what to say. "I—we—wanted you

to hold the baby also, during the ceremony? This is something normal for the grandfather to do."

"During the ceremony?" Lieutenant Donaldson's weight shifted. "You don't mean *while*—?"

Just then, Josef saw six men, led by soldiers, coming from a turn at the other end of the hall. Workers from his kitchen. Including Weber.

Josef looked to the lieutenant.

The lieutenant coughed. "They asked to be here. They like you."

The truth was that most of the people in the town didn't mind them, either. The men worked hard, most of them, and stayed out of trouble. But something was not quite right. About these prisoners—Nazis, really, at least some of them—present at the *bris*. Of Josef's son.

Someone tapped his shoulder.

Nelly. A nurse held the baby behind her.

Nelly's mouth opened and German words, murmured very low, came forth.

"I won't have any Nazis in the room with my son. Especially now. Make them leave," she said. "Please."

"*Liebchen.*" He tightened the prayer shawl. "You said, yourself, they can do nothing to us."

She glanced at the baby and reached for one of his tiny hands. His fingers curled. She closed her own eyes and when she opened them again the ice was melting. No. Michael Jacob—and the voice trembled on the first name, which was her father's—would not be exposed to those, those—.

Lieutenant Donaldson cleared his throat. "I take it there is a problem. I'll just see to it that these—guests—are removed."

Nelly turned away. Josef grasped some of the shawl's fringes in his fist. He almost said something else to her. Almost, he said something else.

But the *mohel* wanted to get on with the event of the day. He explained the covenant. How Abraham circumcised himself, and his son.

"You can circumcise your son, too," he told Josef, smiling. "But there's an escape clause, for you." The men from Omaha laughed.

"Escape?" Josef asked, despite himself, because really he knew that here, now, he had no need to worry about this word.

"You can choose to have me perform this ritual."

"That is why you are here, no?" Everyone laughed. Josef knew that this response was also not quite right. But his greater concern was that Nelly's eyes had once more turned cloudy.

The infant screamed at the moment everyone expected, but the *mohel* put a few extra drops of wine in his little mouth and his cries grew softer. Nelly leaned against the door, then signaled a nurse, and left him, Josef, alone to hear the *mohel* welcome Moshe Yakov ben Yosef to the Jewish community.

Later, maybe, he would explain to the lieutenant that they named Michael Jacob for both his blessed grandfathers. The one died of diabetes. And the one died of Dachau.

Tomorrow, says the doctor, Nelly and the baby leave the hospital. Josef can come fetch them after the breakfast shift. After that, well, the world is open. Free. In America. In Clarinda. The country's basket of bread. How much quiet. How much land.

Homecomings

Nelly Freiburg's mother had brought along few possessions when she escaped Europe; she'd accumulated few others in Brazil, where she had waited out the war, or in Brooklyn, where she had lived an additional quarter-century before taking that final nap on the afternoon of January 10, 1972. So when Nelly made the last trip to the Beth Israel Home for Elders ten days later, she knew a couple of cartons would more than suffice.

In her mother's room, Nelly tucked an afghan into a carton. On top of it she placed the black and white wedding photographs. Her parents, back in Germany. Her own husband, Josef, and herself, surrounded by other refugee friends and relatives in New York, four months after Pearl Harbor. Their son, Mickey, and his Paula, smiling, just six years ago.

Then she turned to the more colorful images of her baby granddaughter — although Rebecca would be

three in June, not such a baby anymore—beribboned
for Rosh Hashanah or Passover. Some photos Nelly had
taped to the wall next to her mother's bed. She peeled
them loose, while she sat on the bare mattress. Something about the task reminded her not to forget the
small brass nameplate, affixed to the door facing the
hallway, spelling SOFIE KAHN. A gift on her mother's
last birthday, from the kids.

Nelly needed two hours to accomplish all this,
but more than two hours, or two weeks, or even two
months, to stop searching for change every morning,
so she might take the bus over to the Home. To remember that she really couldn't just share that bit of
news. To decide where—or even whether—to keep the
nameplate.

For his part, Josef still trudged to the bakery early
each day. At least Mickey and Paula and the little one
lived nearby, and Grandma was the preferred babysit-
ter. Nelly loved nothing more than the feel of Rebecca's small self climbing into her lap, her fingers freely
exploring Nelly's face and the fleshy folds beneath her
chin and arms.

So by late March she might have been feeling better, if not for her birthday—her first as an orphan. But
maybe because that early spring of 1972 marked their
thirtieth wedding anniversary as well, they yielded when

Mickey and Paula insisted that they "really celebrate."

Of course, they all arrived at the restaurant a few minutes early. *Pünktlichkeit.*

"Freiburg, reservation at six-fifteen," Mickey said to the maître d'. "Party of five."

With pleasure Nelly saw other diners pause and smile as Rebecca toddled by, clinging to her mother by one hand and her grandmother by the other. Soon they had arrived at their table and, seated, contemplated the overwhelming menus.

"*Liebchen,* what do I want?" Josef asked her. He'd long since grown accustomed to yielding to her opinions on food and many other matters.

Rebecca banged on the table with her spoon.

"You want steak," Nelly decided. She looked at the waiter. "He wants steak. The T-bone."

"And you'd like that cooked how, sir?"

Josef waited.

"He'd like it medium."

"Medium," Josef repeated.

"Meeed-yum!" Rebecca shrieked, bouncing on her seat. Josef grinned and clapped his hands. Rebecca imitated him.

Mickey frowned. "Calm down, Rebecca." He motioned to his wife. "She's getting all H-Y-P-E-R."

Paula gave him a meaningful look. "She's fine." She set Rebecca's water glass a few inches further out of the child's reach.

The waiter collected the rest of the orders and left them.

"We have a couple of announcements," Mickey began.

"We'll let Rebecca make the first one." Paula smoothed the child's hair and caught her attention. "Sweetie, remember what we practiced? What we said you would tell Grandma and Grandpa?"

The little girl was silent for a moment, then mumbled something incomprehensible. But, like always, Grandma wanted to be encouraging.

"Oh, sweetheart," Nelly said. "That's wonderful!"

Paula smiled. "Did you understand her?"

Josef pointed to the dinner rolls.

Mickey passed his father the breadbasket. "She said, 'I'm going to be a big sister.' That's what she said."

Nelly's memory flashed back to the moment her son and daughter-in-law had announced the first pregnancy, with the family gathered for Rosh Hashanah. Nelly's mother had clasped her hands, her eyes bright. "A baby, a baby," she'd exclaimed. And when Nelly and Josef had brought her, in her wheelchair, to the hospital to see the newborn girl for the first time, the emotion among them had been nearly thick and palpable enough to slice.

Now Paula touched Nelly's hand. "I know how happy Oma Sofie would be," she said, softly.

Nelly reached in her bag for a tissue. Not that she was actually going to cry. "So, when—?" she began.

"November," Mickey said. "Early November."

"Around the time of the election," Paula added. "November 7, the doctor said."

In spite of herself Nelly frowned. She just didn't trust that Richard Nixon. So he'd gone to China. Big deal. As she'd pointed out to Josef, it was such a victory, for the President of the United States to take a trip on his very own airplane?

"And thank *you* for bringing that up," Mickey said. "Anyway, before the world as we know it comes to an end with the likely re-election of Richard Nixon, we want Grandma and Grandpa to take advantage of their special anniversary gift." He handed over what seemed to be a travel folder. Tickets.

"Now that Oma Sofie is—." He had spoken so beautifully at the funeral, but now—although he had been the only grandchild, so loved by, and so loving toward, Sofie Kahn—he could scarcely mention his grandmother. "Well—you should travel. You should go back to Europe."

The waiter brought their salads. Josef lifted his fork.

Mickey had it all planned, he revealed the next day, when he and Nelly talked privately on the phone. He'd corresponded with the cousins in Strasbourg. He'd anticipated all Nelly's objections.

For instance, she said, it was too cold right now.

"Actually," Mickey answered. "It's spring. Warmer every day."

She and Josef would not miss the wedding of their neighbors' daughter.

"That's just a few weeks away."

And they would not miss Rebecca's birthday, either. Never.

"Of course not."

By summer it would be too hot. And Josef had to work.

"The man's entitled to some vacation," Mickey reasoned. "And what better time to break away from that place than summer?"

Didn't Mickey realize how hot it would be in Europe then? No air-conditioning! And so crowded!

"Not at the very end of the summer. Late August. Early September. I hear it's a great time to go."

Finally the words escaped her: "I'm afraid."

He didn't falter. "That's the point. The cousins in Strasbourg will understand. But think of it, Mom. The chance to go back and see your apartment in

Mannheim, and maybe even visit your father's gravesite for the first time." Daniel and Simone would take her and bring her back over the border to France, at night. No one expected her to sleep on German soil.

"Besides," Mickey added. "Germany's going to be full of tourists with the Olympics at the end of the summer. I bet we couldn't even get you a hotel room, now."

She said nothing.

"It'll be good for you," he said. "Closure. Especially now that Oma Sofie—." Again, he stopped.

Closure. What did her twenty-seven-year-old son know about closure? What did that newfangled word mean, anyway? But at times, it was just easier to give in, to be taken care of, to decide that there was no arguing with Mickey. He was smart. He'd gone to college, and to business school. He had those two degrees and a fine job and thanks to him, she and Josef would probably never really have to worry about having food on their table, ever again.

She cleared her throat. "All right," she said. "We'll go."

Mannheim's water tower still stood, surrounded by well-tended lawn. The florist shop she and her father had visited each week, so that he could buy a bouquet for her mother—still there, too. The office where her father had run his business, until the Reich outlawed that. Only the shoe store had changed; now it was a café. The shoe store, where she had found a job at the age of eighteen, because even with her *Abitur* she couldn't attend university. Not then. Not in 1933. But her father had said: "You're not just sitting around here, my dear girl. Waiting to emigrate. You shall do something useful."

Her cousin Daniel turned the Citroën off the city's main ring, onto Ifflenstrasse, and Nelly thought she'd stopped breathing. The building, where she and her parents had lived in an apartment that occupied the entire second floor, was the same! The same purplish stone. The same flowerboxes. The same big windows.

No. The windows. Those were not the same.

"Those men came in," her mother had said, once they could speak freely about that night back in November 1938. "They smashed the windows. The china. The paintings." Much worse, indescribably worse, was the way they had smashed her father, too. Before, even, sending him to Dachau. Today one could visit Dachau, and it seemed that many people were, especially this summer of 1972, since it was a mere six miles from the Olympic Stadium in Munich. There'd even been a memorial service, at that place, with the Israeli athletes laying wreaths. They'd seen the pictures of this event already, and Nelly had stared at the grainy newspaper photographs with some fascination. Still, the thought of going anywhere near there made her retch.

Her cousin slowed the car to a stop and turned to face her. "Shall I see if the current owners are home? Would you like to go inside?"

Nelly pressed on Josef's arm. The air in the car seemed unbearably warm. "The window," she whispered. "Roll it down."

"Honey?" How easily Josef worried. She studied his warm brown eyes. Here, next to her in the back seat of her cousin's Citroën, was someone uneducated, someone uncultured, someone who certainly did not bring her a bouquet every week. They never would have met or married had she stayed here in Mannheim, and had he stayed in his little village on the edge of the Black Forest.

But they'd got out. And in the upside-down world of that time they'd ended up visiting the same friend in the same New York boarding-house. Each, alone. She taught him English. And flowers or not, he was devoted to her. And, in due time, to Mickey. Paula. Rebecca. "Josef would run in front of a truck for any of us," her daughter-in-law had confided, once. It was true.

Nelly's father would have done the same. He hadn't been run over by a truck, though. Not literally.

"We couldn't keep the casket open, when they sent

him back from that place," her mother had said, dry-eyed, after the war. "He was so beaten, so broken. It was better, to keep it closed."

Thus had ended the life of Michael Kahn, for whom a grandson, whom everyone called Mickey, would one day be named. But back in November 1938 there was only a wife, Sofie Kahn, numb in the apartment in Mannheim; a daughter, disbelieving in New York; and a visa application, clogged in the American consulate in Stuttgart.

Nelly turned toward the closed window on her side of the car. She leaned her forehead against the glass and wished, silently, for a glass of water.

"I don't think we'll be contacting those people in the apartment, today," Simone said.

Nelly did not protest as the key turned in the ignition, the engine started, and the wheels scraped against the street.

They hadn't yet crossed back into France. Daniel stopped the car again.

"Need some petrol," he explained. "This is a decent stop."

"I want to buy Rebecca some souvenirs, anyway," Nelly said.

In the small store "MÜNCHEN1972" T-shirts and

banners and magnets abounded.

Nelly considered them all. "Let's buy a bag," she told Josef, examining one in black leather, though its odor only added to her discomfort. "A real keepsake." Not like a T-shirt. She didn't want Rebecca to hate Germany, to hate all Germans. Maybe this new generation could have a new start. In an era when Israeli athletes could be present, marching along with everyone else. In Germany. It was amazing, especially if you remembered Berlin in '36, as Nelly did.

Still, she left it to Josef, to actually reach for the bag. To approach the cashier. To hand the credit card over.

"Maybe we can watch some of the Games, this evening," Josef suggested later.

They did. The next morning Josef asked if they could watch some more. Nelly realized she hadn't yet inquired as to how Josef was feeling, about having been back to Germany, or even whether he had any desire to return to his own hometown. The least she could do was sit and watch those competitions a little longer.

They switched the television on. The screen showed athletes, winning more medals. Sunbathing by the pond. Playing ping-pong.

But there were bulletins. About something else. Something beyond comprehension.

Black September, the group was called. At least one Israeli athlete was dead. No one knew exactly how many were captive in Building 31, in that sunshiny Olympic Village.

Between the competitions—"How can the Games go on like that?"—she and Daniel and Simone kept asking each other, when they could speak at all, and when they weren't mesmerized by the images of trucks marked with the all-too-familiar "POLIZEI" that suddenly seemed to fill Munich's streets—they absorbed the interviews.

Including the one with the Israeli prime minister. More than anything else, more than appearing angry or vindictive or even fearful, Mrs. Meir looked deeply dejected. Grieving. But that old determination showed in her not-altogether downcast eyes when she refused to negotiate with the terrorists.

"If we should give in," she said, her voice steady and sure, no Israeli would be safe. Ever. Anywhere. What had happened to the Israeli team during the night, she declared, what was currently underway, was nothing except "blackmail—of the worst kind."

Simone sighed. "She's right."

Hours passed. Nelly sat on the sofa, sentences coalescing in silence. *It is a Tuesday in September. I am in*

Europe. Two hours from my old home. And the Jews are again the targets.

I have to get out of here.

I have to get out of here.

But instead they continued to sit by the television. Early in the afternoon, Daniel looked over to her.

"Maybe it isn't the right day," he began. "But do you want to see your father's grave? Maybe try the apartment again today, too?"

She shook her head. Because it wasn't the right day.

In the evening, as Simone and her daughter were preparing supper, the phone rang.

"It's for you, Nelly," Simone called from the kitchen. "It's your Michael."

She and Josef exchanged a glance as she hurried to the phone.

"What's wrong?" she asked, before even telling her son hello. She leaned against the wall. "Is Rebecca all right? Paula?"

They were all fine, he said. Why did she always jump to such awful conclusions?

He just wanted to see how the trip was going. He sure hoped she wasn't going to let these "events" in Munich ruin anything.

"Have you been to the grave yet?" he asked.

She hesitated. "No."

Long pause.

"Can you put Rebecca on the phone, please?" she asked.

"She's napping," he said, in a voice that sounded suspiciously short. She still didn't understand his apparent insistence on her revisiting these scenes. These ghosts. But this wasn't the time to explore it.

"How is Paula feeling?" she asked, instead.

"She's fine. She's resting."

"Send our love, then."

She stood for a few moments with her hand on the phone, then returned to Josef. And then she stayed on the sofa, even after the reassuring initial reports, even while the others moved to the table for the meal, because she had a very bad feeling.

Which proved to be justified. Because the Germans, so masterful at murder just a few short decades ago, had truly botched the job at the airport. They'd failed to kill the terrorists. So in the end, in addition to the two dead Israelis back at the Village, the terrorists had, with the help of a grenade and a machine gun, much more effectively ended the lives of the other nine Jews.

The commentators noted that the Games had indeed paused, eleven hours into the siege, and that there would be a memorial service in the morning.

She couldn't go back to Germany. Not then. Not in September 1972.

"I'm not in any shape to handle it," she told Josef. "We'll go another time."

They thanked the cousins, boarded the train to Paris, and flew the Pan Am jet back.

Outside customs, Rebecca stood between her swollen mother and her father.

"*Wie war die Reise?*" Paula asked.

"*Sehr gut!*" Josef said, pleased, as always, when Paula tried a German phrase.

"It was a good trip," Nelly confirmed. "We're very grateful. And we're grateful to be home." She scooped Rebecca into her arms. The child settled against her, as always. Mickey lifted one of the suitcases.

"Do you have everything?" he asked.

The leaves changed. They turned the clocks back. Soon it would be time not just to see Nixon re-elected, but to say *Kaddish* for her father, again. But this fall promised hope and happiness amid the usual dread. Because the baby was due.

"We just want you to know, of course, that we'll take care of Rebecca," Nelly told Mickey and Paula. "When the baby comes."

"We're counting on that," Paula said. "Especially if

I'm induced again. It will be a huge help." She glanced at Mickey.

He cleared his throat. "Yes," he said. "It will." And in a move that seemed to take them all by surprise—even the baby, whose sudden shift must have caused Paula to take that sharp breath and place her hands over her middle—Mickey came over to her, to Nelly, and embraced her.

The morning of the birth Nelly put Rebecca on the bus to her nursery school, then returned to wait by the phone. Which rang shortly after eleven.

"Well, Mom," Mickey said.

"Is everything all right?" So much could go wrong. So much.

"Paula's fine. The baby's fine." His voice shook. "Sofie—Sofie Freiburg—arrived an hour ago. Six pounds, twelve ounces."

"Sofie," she whispered.

"That's right." He exhaled. "Listen, I want to tell Rebecca, myself. Don't tell her, when you pick her up, OK? I'll be over before dinner."

Sofie. Sofie.

She cried, after the phone call, as she opened the drawer she hadn't touched in months, to find a gift for her new grandchild. Another keepsake.

It was buried beneath the afghan and the photographs. The small brass rectangle. She'd check again, about Paula and baby Sofie's homecoming. She'd prepare food, have Rebecca dressed up for a party. How long could it take, to fasten the nameplate?

Or—perhaps she'd wait. What was waiting, anyhow? Why not wait, too, until this Sofie, as well as her sister, could talk and listen and understand? Then she could perhaps give the nameplate over with words to match it.

Or—maybe—there could even be another trip. This time she and Josef wouldn't go on their own; they'd ask Mickey and Paula to come along and to bring the girls. Rebecca, and Sofie. Maybe then she'd be ready, herself, to go back to Mannheim. To the house, and to the grave.

Then again, maybe she would not.

Floating

Everything would be fine.

That's what Mia kept telling herself, while she sat in the breakfast room. Every few seconds she glanced at the phone on the wall. It was better that Jerry had left on his business trip. This way he wouldn't be calling or e-mailing her every five minutes to see if she'd heard anything yet. It was better for her to have the house quiet and calm, better to sense all the cosmic space, clear and clean between this breakfast room and the hotel suite across the continent in California where, hopefully, Jerry still slept.

His absence kept her busier, too. Before settling in at the breakfast room table she'd driven to the newsstand to fetch the papers (a *New York Times* and a *Newark Star-Ledger*), then stopped at the gas station (though the tank wasn't yet half-empty), and even treated herself to a chocolate-coated doughnut (reviving a very long-ago pregnancy habit) at the town deli. Now, at ten minutes to nine, the car gathered frost on the driveway while she was back in the breakfast room, the winter sun streaming in, the *Star-Ledger* atop the *Times* and bearing another front-page story on that poet laureate character, the doughnut uneaten.

Everything would be fine.

Just thirty miles away, at a Manhattan hospital, her daughter and son-in-law were having a "second opinion" test. Her daughter and son-in-law and the thirteen-week-old grandchild whose fetal image as of the previous week (you could see the perfect vertebrae, already, and the little arms and legs!) Mia could spend hours studying on the computer screen. It was a beautiful sonogram.

"Don't you think it looks just like you, Mom?" Mia's daughter had joked, to break the tension. Because as beautiful as the baby was, it was also borderline—as far as its nuchal fold measurement went.

"Its what?" Jerry had asked, more confused than concerned in that first moment when Mia had attempted to discuss the matter. "Noo-cal what? What's that?"

"The skin of its neck," Mia said, trying to sound knowledgeable. She'd looked the term up on the Internet, after her daughter's telephone explanation had raced by too quickly for her to absorb. Jerry still didn't seem to grasp what she was saying, so Mia added, "They can measure it, and if it's too thick, that can be an early

Floating

indication that something isn't quite right. With the baby."

Jerry was silent for a moment. Then he said, "How do you spell it?"

Mia had to admit she hadn't known that initially, herself. "Progesterone" she'd managed well enough, and explained to her husband, when Allison first reported: "I have good news, and some possible bad news," and proceeded to say that she was four weeks pregnant, but that her progesterone level was low, and that her doctor had prescribed supplementary hormones. There might be a miscarriage.

So there was reason to be happy, but not delighted. Not yet.

Then the progesterone levels had risen, and steadied, and they'd all been happier. For awhile.

"We can be cautiously optimistic," they'd agreed.

Cautiously optimistic. A mother expecting her first child wasn't supposed to have to be "cautiously optimistic." She was supposed to celebrate, to revel in the life growing inside her, to glow (like the cliché dictated) and to tell everyone why. Mia wanted to cry. Some days, when she was alone, she did cry, because it worried Jerry too much to see her upset. She was prone to migraines and, before the pacemaker, fainting spells. Any indication of stress and Jerry would start hovering over her. So she kept her unhappinesses to herself, until Jerry left the house.

The house was a five-bedroom colonial, with neat black shutters and a circular driveway, and in truth it was too large for just the two of them, now that Allison and Andrew were grown and out on their own. But it also formed such a part of the life Mia had dreamed of, growing up. One day, she'd fantasized, she'd have a loving husband and a house in the suburbs. And of course, she'd have her children.

They'd married young, she and Jerry, and by their second anniversary they had saved enough to "start trying." They didn't anticipate any difficulties conceiving, and they didn't have any. So later, when she learned of all the miscarriages and fertility treatments and emergency C-sections and other traumas friends and acquaintances had suffered through, and began to have "health issues" herself, she marveled at how easy it had been. Two perfectly planned pregnancies. Two utterly uncomplicated deliveries, beginning with labors that started well after sunrise and had produced living, breathing babies by lunchtime. A daughter, and then, after what she'd understood to be the ideal three-and-one-half-year age difference, a son.

The first pregnancy Mia remembered with a clarity somewhat missing from the second, when she had also simultaneously supervised Allison's tonsillectomy and transition to nursery school and their move to a larger apartment and her own mother's medical care. The first pregnancy belonged to that golden time when life was still so very simple, when she and Jerry lived in a West Side walk-up and didn't even own a car, when so much was still new and unknown, when so much promise filled the future. She was twenty-three years old.

It never occurred to her that everything wouldn't be fine. Back then.

Back then they didn't have nuchal fold tests. They didn't have sonograms. They didn't measure the amount of progesterone in your blood every few days and offer you special treatments in the early weeks of the pregnancy. They didn't have chorionic villus sampling; she could only vaguely recall hearing, back then, the term "amniocentesis." But that was for much older women. Wasn't it?

She'd gone to the doctor—Jerry's aunt with the four children still at home had given her the name of her own obstetrician. Dr. Grossman, a middle-aged man with a crowded waiting room, had spent five minutes examining her and said, "Yes, honey, you're pregnant. I don't even need to see the test results." He'd asked about her last cycle, then told her the baby's due date. And she'd reported it all to her husband, right away.

"I floated out of that office," she told Allison, many times, recounting the wonder of that first pregnancy. "Daddy and I were just floating, for the next eight months before you came. Not a care in the world."

Were they just ignorant back then? Was it so wrong to assume that without thalidomide or DES in your history you didn't need to worry? "Didn't you even consider Tay-Sachs?" Allison had asked, and Mia had to confess that no, she hadn't. But Allison was undergoing every test imaginable. In fact, insurance had refused to pay for some of the sonography.

Mia separated the newspapers. She couldn't handle the impending war and other disasters no doubt filling the *Times*, not when there might be another crisis coming through the phone lines at any moment. But the *Star-Ledger*'s front-page focus on the latest poet laureate problem made her massage her temples, too. At least, with everything else to talk about today, it was unlikely that Allison would start in on that whole subject again.

"She really should have gone to law school," Jerry said, frequently, about their management-consultant daughter. "Since she's so fond of prosecuting everyone and everything."

Mia left the breakfast table, headed to the computer down the hall. She clicked onto the most recent sonogram and studied the picture of her grandchild, a grainy figure floating in its dark sac. The tears pooled and pressed.

Why hadn't they called yet? The appointment was for 8 a.m. Surely they knew something by now.

For God's sake, her daughter deserved to float, too!

True, Mia had actually appeared rather weightless back then.

"You must be pregnant," Jerry had said, his voice gaining energy, as they dined on hot dogs at Nathan's the evening before that first visit to Dr. Grossman. (Who knew about nitrites?) "Because I've never seen you finish a meal before!"

She'd been so thin, in fact—barely 100 pounds when she'd first conceived—that she'd not only sworn that she felt Allison move in the fourth month, but to her delight she'd soon seen the little knees and elbows protruding through her skin. At night she and Jerry would lie on their bed and watch the baby shift in her body, mesmerized.

"It's floating around," she'd say, stunned at what was happening within her. As if no one else on the planet had ever experienced such a thing.

And she'd gained just fourteen pounds that entire pregnancy, because Dr. Grossman was—well, to put it nicely—something of an ogre; she and all the other women in that waiting room were so frightened of his scoldings about weight gain that they essentially starved themselves before each weigh-in. After the appointments, she'd cross the street and find other mothers-to-be in the coffee shop, shoveling food down their throats.

Her own preference was chocolate-coated doughnuts, but the others seemed to favor mocha layer cake, or apple pie.

Allison hated chocolate-coated doughnuts.

Allison's obstetrician had an office on Park Avenue.

Jerry had given Mia a rueful look. "I wonder what multiple of Grossman's fee he charges."

"*She* charges," Allison corrected. "And hello! It is thirty-three years later!"

Everything would be fine. The obstetrician and technicians would give them the assurances they needed. And then they could tell the rest of the family, the cousins and the close friends who were like extra siblings and aunts and uncles.

After Mia's first visit with Dr. Grossman, after she'd floated out of that office and told Jerry that her suspicions had been confirmed, they could barely wait until dinner. They'd gone over that Friday night, as planned—as usual, for the Sabbath—but for the first time greeted Jerry's parents with a "Nice to see you, Grandma and Grandpa!" And there'd been pure, joyful laughter, as the realization hit first Jerry's mother, always alert to anything medically-related, and then his father. Pure delight. Absolute and unadulterated happiness. Her husband's parents had fled Hitler back in the 1930s. Jerry was their only son. This baby—and its future sibling—would be the center of their lives, until the days Grandpa and then Grandma had died, many many years later.

"*L'chaim!*" Mia's father-in-law had shouted, lifting a glass of Manischewitz Concord Grape.

To life. It was a time they had thought of nothing but new life. No illness. No defects. No calamities or crises. Because back then everyone was healthy and alive.

After dinner with her in-laws she and Jerry had dropped by her mother's apartment.

"This is a surprise," her mother had said. "Weren't you coming tomorrow?"

And then, in a microsecond, Mother had seen their smiles and let out a shriek.

"You're expecting!"

Next to know were Mia's own brother and sister-in-law, themselves already waiting for their second child. Mia recalled the sense of familial love and warmth enveloping her from that moment on, just like the sheets and blankets that wrapped her in the most peaceful sleep of her life, all through that pregnancy. Never again would she sleep so well, and not only because babies could keep parents awake.

Thirty-something years later her mother was dead.

So were Jerry's parents. Her brother's wife was gone, too—breast cancer. And now Mia's nights were punctuated with those moments when she awoke and wondered how to help her brother through his own treatment. The prostate. Good news carried so much more responsibility, these days. So many burdens. Because floating was so much more elusive in this life, with the holes of loss and absence, the demands of replacement, the trials and terrors tearing through the hours and days and years.

She returned to the breakfast room, to the doughnut and the newspapers. In the *Times* she skimmed the world news, the weather, the obituaries. And then she dared to read the *Star-Ledger*.

"N.J. Senate Votes To Eliminate Poet Laureate Post."

This she must absorb, as Allison was obsessed with the issue.

"It's outrageous," her daughter had said, when the kids came in for the weekend of Jerry's birthday in October (Andrew had even brought a new girlfriend), and they'd all sat around this very table, with bagels and lox and the Sunday *Times*, and Allison had gone straight for the Week in Review. The new girlfriend, though likely warned, still seemed slightly nonplussed by Allison's intensity.

"What's outrageous?" the poor girl had asked.

"Here we go," Andrew said. "Anyone want more coffee? Or a tranquilizer?"

Allison's husband laughed. Jerry frowned.

"You don't know about the poet laureate?" Allison's eyebrows raised. And then she'd explained the situation. How in a poem this man had perpetuated a conspiracy theory that Israelis—read, Jews—knew in advance of the September 11 attacks.

"Never mind that hundreds of Jews were among the people killed that day," Allison said.

Allison's husband sighed.

The new girlfriend looked at Andrew. "What did the poem say?"

"I'm sure Allison can quote it for you."

"Not quite." Allison glared at her brother. "But almost." She addressed the girlfriend again. "One line suggests someone warned 'Israeli workers' at the Towers not to go in that day. And another implies there's something fishy about Ariel Sharon being off-site, too." She shook her head, while her brother's girlfriend's expression seemed to freeze halfway between bewilderment and terror. "Can't imagine why Sharon wouldn't have been there. I mean, he only runs another country in an entirely different part of the world."

"Doesn't this man—this poet—have the right to express himself?" Andrew asked.

"Does anyone want another bagel?" Mia broke in. "Toasted?"

"Well, I like to think that something others might read as historical truth is at least quasi-accurate, but let's put that aside, because I know you'll just tell me,"— and indeed, Andrew's mouth had opened—"that 'truth' is a subjective concept." Allison paused, and Andrew's mouth shut.

"So sure, let him express himself—but I'd prefer that as a representative of the state, especially, he not do it quite this way. And not on taxpayer money," Allison continued. "Which, please forgive me for pointing out, Mr. ACLU, but in this county, in particular, happens to include a lot of Jewish taxpayer money. You think Mom and Dad really want to be, for all intents and purposes, funding anti-Semitic propaganda?"

"Allie—" her husband interrupted. Or tried to.

But she was on a roll. Refocusing on Mia, as if she knew it would be hopeless to try to politicize her father, she demanded: "I mean, aren't you upset that your taxes are going to support this man? And that he's spouting such poison—really dangerous poison—so nearby?" For Newark, where this poet was now preaching and teaching in the schools, was their own county seat.

Mia had felt another migraine coming on.

"Allison, for God's sake," Jerry had pleaded. "Leave your mother alone!"

The phone rang. Mia stood, too quickly. Usually the pacemaker regulated her heartbeat, but now she felt light-headed. She held onto the back of her chair. She must not collapse. That was all she needed—another episode for Jerry to worry over. The answering machine clicked on. Allison was speaking but Mia couldn't distinguish the words. Again tears blurred her vision. All she could hear was her father-in-law's voice, all she could see was his still-familiar smile.

L'chaim!

The machine clicked off. Mia steadied herself and made her way over to the message. Everything would be fine. Just fine.

Wouldn't it?

The Quiet American, or
How to Be a Good Guest

You will go to Germany. You will go, after years and years of refusing to go (even when you traveled through the rest of Europe after your freshman year of college), just as you refused to learn German until circumstances (that is to say, graduate school requirements) forced you to. But if your grandparents, may they rest in peace, managed to go back and visit, way back in 1972, then you can go. You will be practically next door in beautiful baroque Central Europe for a conference; you really should go while someone else has paid your transatlantic airfare. So you will.

You are an American. You are a grown-up. What's to worry about? Even now, even this summer of 2004, when your own homeland needs security, and every time you watch the news you're afraid you'll hear about another suicide bombing on a bus in Israel.

You talk with your best friend before you leave. You

say: "I don't know which is worse, at this point. To be an American in Europe—or to be a Jew."

Your best friend is also an American Jew. She also has European-born grandparents. Hers survived a total of seven camps. Your best friend doesn't have an answer.

So today, a hot Sunday in August—a very hot Sunday that reminds you how much you hate extremes in anything, especially the weather—you are in Stuttgart. This is the city to which each of your father's parents had traveled from their hometowns, back in the late 1930s, to apply for their visas at the American Consulate. You've already searched the Web and thumbed through the local telephone directory in your nice, air-conditioned hotel room.

There is no longer an American Consulate in Stuttgart.

When you were younger, your parents and you and your sister went to Paris. Because even then you showed an appalling inability to read a map and you demonstrated a similarly instinctive lack of any sense of direction, your parents signed you all up for a family bus tour of the city. Jet-lagged, you fell asleep two minutes into the tour, by the Place de la Concorde.

But twenty years later you are in Stuttgart, and you aren't jet-lagged, and your parents have reminded you, via an e-mail message that you read at a cybercafe, that it would be a good idea to take a bus tour of the city. To orient yourself. So you have already visited the information office at Königstrasse 1A to learn about the tours. You've paid your seventeen euros and bought your ticket. And now you are standing outside the Hotel am Schlossgarten, waiting for the bus.

You aren't jet-lagged, but you do have a cold, and every few moments you sneeze and blow your nose into tissues you then stuff into your bag. Probably this will guarantee an empty seat next to you, for which you are grateful. You can identify the other Americans easily enough—although somewhat atypically you can't instantly guess whether they are American Jews or Gentiles—and your instincts are affirmed when you casually step closer and overhear their conversation.

English. American English.

When you climb on the nice, air-conditioned bus you sit behind them.

All the other passengers seem to be German. And old. The natural question comes to mind as the bus lumbers along: *What did they do during the war?* Maybe your mind is playing tricks on you but somehow the old women across the aisle bear a striking resemblance to your grandmother: fleshy and white-haired with proud noses and blue-gray eyes.

Your guide—an unusually petite woman named Greta who is wearing a string of green beads and whose lined face suggests she might be in her fifties, like your parents—lets forth a stream of words in German and then she says, in English, that this is how she runs things: she will tell the group everything in German and then repeat it for the English-speakers. You smile. You've already forgotten nearly all the German you learned that summer you needed to acquire proficiency for graduate school.

Except for one word. And it's not a day of the week or a month of the year or a color or anything so simple.

It's *Vergangenheitsbewältigung*. It's a word that means, roughly, "coming to terms with the past."

Greta with the green beads seems to be a good guide. She tells you that more than five hundred thousand people reside in Stuttgart; she praises its many parks, its ballet, its zoo. She describes all the buildings the bus passes. The State Gallery. The Opera House. The regional Parliament Building.

As the tour continues there's a refrain. Again and again Greta says: "This building had to be rebuilt after the war. The original was destroyed by the bombings."

Is that a note of accusation in her voice? Or are you just being, as you've been told you can be, paranoid?

The Americans—you and the American family occupying two rows across from you whom by now you've learned live in Chicago—say nothing. Naturally. You're all just guests, here. The teenage son in the Chicago group dons some headphones and his parents don't say anything then, either, not even, *We paid seventeen euros for you to go on this bus trip and you're going to listen to what the guide has to say!* Maybe they don't want him to listen, anymore. In the meantime, his sister reaches for some bottled water.

But a few rows ahead someone is shaking his shiny bald head, every time Greta makes that comment about the buildings and the bombings. The white-haired woman sitting next to him doesn't move.

Part of you is actually sympathetic to Greta. You've read Günter Grass's *Crabwalk*. You've read W.G. Sebald's essay "Air War and Literature." You understand that the Germans suffered, too. The civilians. Maybe Greta's family suffered. Maybe Greta's father or uncle or older brother was gravely injured or even killed on the Eastern Front. You could understand, if that were her point.

The problem—and it's a serious problem—is that that doesn't seem to be her point. Buildings don't quite equal civilian lives, but buildings seem to be what preoccupy your tour guide. But you stay quiet. You shred a tissue and drop the pieces into your bag. You pick at your cuticles and at the chipped polish on your fingernails. Because, again, you might just be paranoid.

But you also stay quiet because, remember, you are a guest. And not just any guest. You're one who just doesn't know whether it's worse to be an American or a Jew in Europe these days. And today you aren't only in Europe.

You are in Germany.

But Greta the Guide won't give up. Now you're looking at the New Palace. It's really an old palace; in fact, it's a very old palace. But it, too, suffered tremendously during the war, the poor thing. You've descended from the bus, all of you, to admire it close-up. The Germans heard the story first, and now they've walked off, across the street, to await the guide at the next landmark while you and your compatriots get the English version. To your surprise the bald man and the white-haired woman, whom you had taken for an old German couple, remain with your Anglophone group. Greta speaks.

Another tale of destruction. Another refrain. Again you're hearing that line about how much work had to be done to repair this building postwar, because "the original was destroyed by the bombings."

Now you're getting really annoyed. And you're standing in the sun and sniffing away, to boot. But you'd be annoyed anyway.

As a Jew. Because this woman—this so-called

guide—seems to be privileging certain kinds of wartime destruction over others, and her judgment is more than a little bit warped, in your opinion.

And as an American. Because you can't help feeling that this woman is angry at the Allies for having "destroyed" her country's property. Apparently there's no credit in the Bank of Greta's goodwill for the Marshall Plan.

But you say nothing. You think that even Sebald and Grass would want to slap this woman. But you certainly do not slap her. You don't even say anything to her. You are only a guest. So you say nothing. You look away for a moment. Just a few yards from this spot there's a café, where lots of people sit under umbrellas. They're laughing, talking, eating, drinking. They're not standing out here in the sun listening to nonsense and sniffing, now, for multiple reasons. You sigh.

But when you look back at your own little group the bald man is breathing fast. Sweat runs down his face. His wife's freckled hand rests on his arm. You're alarmed. Is there a doctor here? How do you say, "Emergency!" in German? Right now that has to be a word far more important to know than *Vergangenheitsbewältigung.*

But the man shakes free from his wife's grasp. He wipes his face with a white handkerchief. He breathes deeply. And then he starts speaking.

"Young woman," he says to Greta, and you hear at

once the voice of a Briton. Your mind flashes back to the D-Day celebrations that you watched on television at the beginning of the summer while you babysat your toddler niece, major celebrations this year for the sixtieth anniversary of the Normandy landings. "Look, sweetie," you'd said, to this child named for your German-born grandmother, and how proud you'd been when the little girl had stopped strangling her plush stuffed puppy to stand at attention on her chubby legs, solemn-faced and respectfully silent not when George Bush was speaking, not even when the cameras shifted to the display of the Franco-German rapprochement at Caen, but just when the British veterans—an even smaller group than the ever-shrinking pool of American ones—had been marching, in uniform, past Her Royal Majesty Queen Elizabeth II, at Arromanches. In her own way, the queen was a veteran herself, staying in London with her parents and sister throughout it all. They'd been bombed, too, remember.

This British man evidently remembers. He remembers a lot of things.

The sun is in your eyes, and you can't quite look at him right now, but you can hear everything he is saying to the tour guide. "You should think a bit more before you speak, you know. I spent the war in the RAF. I cannot say that I am responsible for these particular bombings to which you continue to refer. But if I were,

I would hardly be ashamed."

Greta stares. Despite the sun, you raise your eyes and stare, too. The Chicagoans—including the headphoned teenager—stare. Everyone stares. Except the Briton's wife, who is rummaging in her large purse.

But no one says anything.

Then you sneeze, and you reach for another tissue. The Briton's wife pulls a cap from the purse and passes it to her husband.

At the end of the tour you give Greta a tip, which she will share with the driver, and you nod your appreciation. It's the polite thing to do. You learned this from your father, when you saw him hand a few coins over to the tour guide on the bus that day twenty years ago, in Paris.

Outside, you hurry to catch up with the bald Briton and his wife. Now you don't have to be so quiet, and you can be more sincere. You have something to say.

"Excuse me," you begin, once you've reached them. And you look at this man, who may not have bombed this city but almost certainly bombed others. You clear your throat. And you speak again.

"Thank you," you say. "Thank you—so much."

Mishpocha

Today, his mother died. Or was it yesterday? David no longer knew how many hours had elapsed since he'd been in his office, speaking with one of the paralegals, when his BlackBerry buzzed, and he recognized the New York City area code but not the number that accompanied it, and a stranger's voice said, "Mr. Kaufmann? I'm calling from Mount Sinai Hospital, and I am sitting here with your father. He's fine." As fine as a man can be once his wife of sixty years returns from a trip to the grocery store, collapses in the kitchen of their apartment, fails to regain consciousness, and is rushed to a hospital, where she continues breathing only because she has been connected to machines.

It would take time to reach the Upper East Side of Manhattan from Center City Philadelphia, that much David was able to reason after the stranger passed the phone to David's father.

"I'll call Amanda and ask her to stay with you until

I can get there, Dad," David promised. He knew he could count on his daughter to taxi uptown at once. His fingers shook as he pressed the preprogrammed number, not knowing how to say what needed to be said once Amanda answered.

Mercifully, she understood. "I'll see you there," she said. "And I'll call Mom, so you can just get going." Mom—David's wife, Barbara—was halfway across the country at a conference of fellow art historians. "And Jon, too," Amanda promised. Her brother, younger by two years, was a senior at Brandeis. There was no one else to inform. David was an only child; he had no living aunts or uncles. Briefly, he considered calling his rabbi. But it seemed he might be calling Rabbi Greenberg soon enough. For now, that call could wait.

He'd never quite remember the drive. All he'd recall was that one minute he was standing in the garage where he parked each day after driving in from the suburbs, holding the briefcase in which he'd had the presence of mind to throw a copy of the health proxy he'd had his mother sign ten years earlier after a particularly gut-wrenching case one of his partners had handled, and then his mind blurred, as did the windshield, and the Volvo steered and EZ-passed itself through a series of tolls, and then he was back in the city of his boyhood, New York, New York.

There was something surreal about driving on a sunny October afternoon on his way to what was almost certainly going to be the darkest moment of his life. This was New York City, with busses and taxis and cars like David's clogging the streets, with stores and restaurants and Starbucks packed together to line the sidewalks, with apartment buildings reaching into the sky. With woefully inadequate parking. But near the hospital there were indeed garages, and David left the car in one and walked, fast, to the correct entrance, while he placed another call to his daughter.

"Nothing's changed, Dad," she said. David should come right on up. Jon would arrive by six. Barbara would land at eight.

Mount Sinai Hospital. How many hospitals outside Israel maintained elevators that automatically stopped on each floor on the Sabbath, when Jews were not allowed to do any work, even if that work involved nothing more than pressing a numbered button on a panel? This hospital did, at any rate, and maybe that was why David felt some small sense of comfort on that short trip up. There was no purpose in trying to move his mother to the amenity floor. She wouldn't be here long enough to benefit from the luxury room, the private chef, the wireless access. Unless he'd gravely misunderstood the situation, he and his wife and children were gathering here to say good-bye. This much, again, the practical, lawyerly part of his self understood.

At the doorway to his mother's room, he paused to glimpse his daughter, auburn-haired and paler than usual, sitting beside his father. Amanda held one of his father's hands; with the other, his father was stroking his mother's arm.

Amanda glanced up. She whispered to her grandfather, who looked up as well.

"David, my son," his father said, removing his eyeglasses and pressing his hands over his eyes.

Amanda stood and within seconds had wrapped her arms around David. "Let me tell the doctor that you're here," she said. David nodded. "And are you sure I can't get you something to eat, Grandpa? Or a drink—coffee?—at least?"

His father shook his head. David took his daughter's seat. His father leaned even closer to the bed. "Esther. Esther, David is here. Can you open your eyes?"

Wasn't this moment almost preordained? Hadn't it been written, somewhere, that this day would come, or some day like it, with one parent in the process of leaving this life, leaving this earth, and the other one left alone by David's side? And hadn't he been through it already, as a witness, at any rate, watching Barbara's father weaken until he could weaken no more? Didn't he know what to expect?

None of that mattered. Because when it happens to you—when it is *your* mother lying there on that bed, reactionless, and *your* father trying to be brave, for *you*, you suspect, for *your* children, the grandchildren he loves so much—you don't know what to do or say.

"I'm going to leave you two alone," his father said, gripping the sides of his chair for leverage.

David found his father's cane, helped him stand. His father was about five inches shorter than David; today, he looked even smaller. David almost said, *Don't go!* Because he knew why his father was leaving the room. To allow David to say good-bye.

His mother's hands rested on the sheets. David was afraid to lift them, worried he might dislodge the tubes and wires. But he had to touch her. He wondered what the EMTs, and then the ER personnel, and then the floor nurses had thought, when they'd seen the numbers on her arm. What questions they'd had. Here they were, David and his mother, at the end, and there were still so many questions. Not that he hadn't tried to get the answers.

Sure, it would have been easier if his parents had spoken about their experiences. Or at least, simply told him about their childhoods before everything went so terribly wrong. If they'd filled him in on the stripped-bare branches of the Kaufmann and Rozenblat family trees instead of leaving it all for him to pursue and piece together later. But it seemed that for his parents—for his mother, especially—life began with David. She remembered all his teachers' names (from kindergarten forward); the date he'd lost his first tooth (February 11, 1960); the details of his worst fever (105.1 degrees—he was three years old); the type of flowers he'd chosen the first time he'd brought her a bouquet for Mother's Day (yellow roses); and the color of the dress Barbara had worn the first time David brought her to his parents' apartment (also yellow). But whenever David tried to go back, even to a time after the Worst, to the years between his parents' departure from Europe and his birth Over Here, she closed up. "David, please leave it all alone," she'd say. His father followed her lead. "David, my son, listen to your mother." Eventually, David had stopped asking. Now, he'd no longer have the chance.

What he did say to her in those moments they had alone, before Amanda and his father returned, before Jon arrived, and then Barbara, and the hours ticked by and the doctors and nurses stopped in and checked his mother and it became clear that nothing was changing, nothing would be better, it was all just as he'd heard from the beginning, and it was a matter of saying goodbye, all of them, and being prepared for the next steps, and especially because he had the papers right there, right with him, with his mother's signature, what he said was simple. That he loved her. That it was OK for her to go. He said that, even though it wasn't OK. Because this much, he knew, was expected. He wasn't supposed to make her fight on. Not this time.

So he did it. At some point, his son arrived, and then his wife. They, too, said their good-byes, and at some strange hour between night and day it was over, and the living Kaufmanns left the hospital together.

"I'll drive," Barbara said. "You're in no shape to do it."

They offered his father the front seat, of course, and, for once, Max Kaufmann accepted it without protest.

Rabbi Michael Greenberg had met David's parents many times, on the Holy Days and at the occasional congregational *seder* they had all attended when David and his wife weren't hosting Barbara's extended family or traveling to one of her sisters' homes, and when Amanda and Jon had been called to the pulpit when they turned thirteen.

"I'm glad to see you again, Mr. Kaufmann," he said to David's father, who'd risen from the sofa to shake the rabbi's hand. "Although, of course, I'm sorry about the circumstances."

"Thank you, Rabbi." David's father swayed slightly. Barbara grabbed his arm.

"Dad, we can handle this," she said. "Let's get you some rest." And to David's surprise, again, his father allowed Barbara to guide him upstairs.

Rabbi Greenberg explained that he'd appreciate

hearing more about Mrs. Kaufmann, to help him prepare remarks for the funeral. He removed a small note-
book from his jacket pocket and uncapped a pen. Then
he waited, perhaps, David thought, remembering the
silence with which David had, on his parents' behalf,
met the suggestion that the children's grandparents address the congregation's religious school classes for *Yom
Hashoah*, Holocaust Remembrance Day.

Amanda broke the silence. "My dad's really the family historian," she said. "He should fill you in."

That was true. David was indeed the family historian. An athlete, he was not. An artist, no. But a good
husband and father—yes. A devoted son—absolutely.
A skilled lawyer, a competent Mr. Fix-it, a decent cook.
Yes, yes, yes. And once his children had left the house
and this magnificent, if still somewhat mysterious cre-
ation called the Internet had clearly arrived on the scene
to stay, his longtime genealogical research hobby gathered more of his attention, and much more momen-
tum.

Each evening he settled at the computer lodged in
one corner of their big, bright, Bosch-equipped kitchen
to read the messages from his discussion groups. He
belonged to the main JewishFamHist.com mailing list,
but he also subscribed to a number of specialty threads:
the German-Jewish FamHist list (his father came from

Germany); the Gesher-Galicia FamHist list (his mother had been born in a village within the landscape now classified as southern Poland and western Ukraine); the Second Generation FamHist list for the children of survivors. Fortunately, he subscribed to each list in digest form. Otherwise, he'd have had hundreds of individual messages flooding his inbox daily.

He didn't need a psychiatrist to explain why this activity so attracted him ("obsessed" was the word that Barbara used to describe it). When most of your family has been—there's no easy way to say it—*exterminated*; when to the question, "How did your parents meet?" you must reply, if you are to be truthful, that their fingers had quite literally entwined over a soup kettle at a European DP camp in 1945, and somehow (they didn't like to talk about it) they'd soon married and then immigrated to New York; when you've had no one to call Grandma or Grandpa, no true aunts or uncles or cousins, you're bound to have questions.

But that didn't mean your parents would provide answers. Instead, from your mother, you heard, "David, please leave it all alone." And from your father, "David, my son, please listen to your mother."

For a while, he'd obeyed. Sort of. He'd stopped asking them directly and had tiptoed instead into that brave new world of the Internet. And yet, despite his own interest, David had been slow to come to the specifically Shoah-related databases. How preferable it was to search for his mother's family in the 1929 Polish Business Directory database, or within the appropriate birth or marriage records indexed online. How much more pleasant—or at least less disturbing—to find burial records for the Kaufmanns dating from Before, than thinking about the deaths that came During. How much easier.

And he had researched Barbara's family. They had proven far easier to trace; since no one else had seemed interested he had taken on the job. This way, his children would know such a lot about half their heritage that, just maybe, the lack of information on the other side wouldn't matter so much. It had been relatively simple to establish that yes, his wife's German ancestors had settled in Philadelphia in the 1830s. All kinds of vital records, in clear and modern English, testified to their place in the world, their role in history. They'd fought for the United States in the Civil War and in World War I, in World War II and in Korea. (Vietnam was another story, with the cousin who'd fled to Canada.) They'd left photographs. They appeared in wedding and birth and death announcements in several American newspapers. Popped up in all kinds of property, probate, and census records. Alumni records, too. David still remembered the awe that filled him during his first visit to Barbara's grandparents' vacation home. It wasn't just the fact that his new girlfriend's grandparents *owned* the rambling house and all that waterfront property that had stunned him. Most amazing was the set of college yearbooks he'd found stored sloppily on a bookshelf, replete with photographs of Barbara's grandfather and grandmother at their respective schools, looking as though they'd stepped directly from the pages of *The Great Gatsby*. All this was one-half of his children's inheritance.

When, at last, he ventured into the world of Holocaust research, he'd stayed general for months. He might explore the databases, for instance, but he wouldn't search for his parents within them. It seemed a big enough step when he managed to read through the offerings on a site titled "Holocaust Database Collection." The first time David had arrived on its homepage, he'd shuddered. "This database incorporates over 120 datasets, listed below." You could find quite a lot there. Jews who resided in Krosno, Poland, before 1941. Polish Martyred Physicians. Jewish Survivors Listed in a Hungarian Periodical. Danish Deportees Database. Arrivals to Buchenwald. Deaths in Mühldorf. Auschwitz-Sachsenhausen Transfers. Surviving Jews in Kielce District. Jews Murdered Near Sabac, Serbia—this last set, David read, would provide data on more than one thousand members of a Zionist youth group who were murdered, together. Which made him think instantly of his daughter, marching with friends in a Salute to

Israel parade. The lists went on and on. Variations on a single, sickening theme.

There was no question that it was thanks to the facts revealed to him on his computer screen that he'd learned some of what his parents had concealed. From the lists of transports, and records of prisoners arriving at camps, and (the much shorter) lists of prisoners liberated from camps, and, at last, United Nations documents on the DPs, he'd discovered the broad outlines of what they'd experienced and could envision just a little more clearly what they had endured. But nothing had helped him solve the puzzle he'd sensed within himself for so long. Even the details he'd discovered about his parents didn't quiet the questioning, the yearning to know who they were before he knew them, before they were his parents, when their definition of family did not yet include him.

If the other members of his Second Generation on-line discussion group did not share his exact concerns they did, to be sure, provide a comfortable familiarity in their interests and perspectives. He rarely posted anything; he hadn't even submitted an introduction until he'd already subscribed to the list for seven months, and then he'd revealed little: "My name is David Kaufmann. I grew up in New York City. My parents, Max and Esther (*née* Rozenblat) Kaufmann met in Deggendorf." Then he listed the camps where each had been a pris-

oner before landing in Deggendorf. And he'd been welcomed, with posts of greeting and sometimes backchan-
neled messages detailing possible ties—a father who'd
also been at Auschwitz; a mother who'd also survived
Sachsenhausen.

In time, he found safety on this list. Here, one
could ask and answer freely. Here, one might even express thoughts impermissible elsewhere. "Look at all
this talk about the Mexicans," one person wrote, an-
guished annoyance in his words. "Why didn't the *Jews*
illegally immigrate?" And another list member's instant
answer: "Too law-abiding." Or a different post, from
someone whose father's family had lived in what was
now Ukraine: "They'd seen others flee from the Germans; their own city was filled with refugees. Why, oh
why didn't they flee when the Germans were on their
doorstep?" And a response: "It was their *home*. What
can move you to leave your home?" And a confidence
shared those summer weeks when the rockets rained on
northern Israel: "I talked with my uncle in Haifa this
morning. He said, 'You know, they faulted us for going like sheep to the slaughter, and now they fault us
for defending ourselves.'" David didn't know why, exactly, but as he kept checking in and reading posts, as
he sensed the palpable emotion on the screen when, in
one case, "We've found my aunt!" and in another, dev-
astating if definitive news about an uncle was learned,

he wanted to know. More.

But he'd let it go. He'd stayed quiet and refrained from asking his parents. And now his mother was dead, and they were sitting there in his living room with Rabbi Greenberg, and he was unable to tell the man the full story of Esther Kaufmann's life.

Somehow, David got through it. They all got through it—the funeral, and the burial, and the days and nights of people coming to the house. Everyone brought food, or so it seemed, and David wondered why it was important. To eat.

He knew what the statistics said: that before a year had passed, he might be right back in his platter-filled dining room, surrounded by all the very same people, reconvened because, lacking the sustaining presence of his spouse, David's father would not survive. This, David tried not to think about.

But something they did think about, and act on, was moving his father closer. Rabbi Greenberg helped them locate Wynnewood, "a first-rate place," in the rabbi's view. And David's father didn't protest the suggestion either, didn't object to anything on the tour, didn't argue when David made all the arrangements for the move, which took place midwinter.

"*I* wouldn't mind living here," Barbara had said, when they took that first tour. And she was right, David thought each time he exited the elevator and started the walk down to his father's corner room. A clean, well-lighted place. Activities galore. It was luxurious ("Dad, I am so glad I can do this for you," he'd managed to say, when they'd first brought his father here, and his father had looked right back at him, eyes bright). And best of all, it didn't smell anything like a nursing home. How the hell did they manage that?

Time passed. The first Passover without his mother. The first what-would-have-been-his-mother's-birthday. David's own birthday, the first without an acknowledgment from the woman who had given him life. The first Mother's Day he didn't have a mother to call or send roses. And then it was summer.

They were going to meet up, a cluster within the Second Generation online discussion group, at the annual Jewish-American Genealogy Conference. For years, David had avoided this conference. It was so much safer to investigate from a distance, far less threatening to keep these connections within this odd little computer-driven community. Besides, the event invariably fell sometime in August when Barbara had negotiated their time at the beach house, or when his son or daughter or both had to be packed up and deposited, or redeposited, at college.

But this year was different. This year they had no kids in college. Jon had just graduated and was spending the summer strengthening his language skills on a kibbutz *ulpan* before beginning a fellowship year at the Hebrew University in Jerusalem. Somehow, Barbara had scheduled them for ten days at the beach that didn't conflict with the conference. And this year the meeting would be held in New York. It wasn't as though he'd have to fly to San Francisco or Seattle. Because frankly, with everything going on in the world these days, who needed to take extra risks like getting on a cross-continental airplane.

Most of all, this was the year his mother had died. This year, David really didn't have to leave it all alone. And he missed her so much. Perhaps going to this conference might restore to him some pieces of her life.

Moreoever, after all this time, David was despite himself more than mildly interested in meeting his Internet colleagues, especially those from the Second Generation discussion group. Part of the conference would focus on genealogy search tips and techniques designed especially for people like them, people whose family trees had been axed away. He'd already highlighted those seminars in the program: Using the Yad Vashem Database. Researching at the U.S. Holocaust Memorial Museum Library. New Possibilities in Postwar Immigration Research. Not to mention those general sessions that might prove particularly helpful, such as Locating Your *Mishpocha* on the Internet: New Sites and Sources.

Thus the third weekend in August had found David and his wife in Manhattan. They'd gone to a concert Barbara selected at Carnegie Hall on Friday night; a play she'd wanted to see for months on Saturday. For Sunday brunch, they'd met Amanda at one of the innumerable diner-coffee shops he still preferred to the more glamorous places he could now afford. Then Amanda had left them, and he and Barbara walked together, holding hands, across the Upper East Side, strolling down the townhouse-lined side streets, toward Fifth Avenue, toward the Metropolitan Museum of Art, where Barbara would spend the rest of the day, and where he'd catch a bus to take him to the conference midtown.

"I'd say that I hope you find what you're looking for," Barbara told him, with an indecipherable smile, after she'd given him a good-bye peck. "But I don't know if you even know what that is."

"Well, we'll see," he said, vaguely. And then, with his own small smile: "You know where everything is—just in case."

She sighed. After thirty years of marriage, and David's more recent nonstop monitoring of the Mideast situation since Jon's departure for Israel, she surely knew this half-joke all too well. That what he was telling her with those few words was this: *I am heading straight into an ideal terrorist target. A Jewish-American genealogy conference, a meeting of hundreds (thousands?) of Jews from all over the world, united in one convenient, commercial location—a sprawling convention hotel in the heart of midtown Manhattan, right there in Times Square. How could any self-respecting terrorist resist the temptation?* It was possible, David had considered, that by going to this conference he was sealing his own death warrant. Somehow, even after 9/11 had "destroyed their innocence," or whatever popular nonsense about Americans' so-called "sense of security" and "inviolability" so many of the newspapers and broadcasts had spewed at that terrible time, he bet that the Gentiles didn't have worries like these when they met for their conferences, in Salt Lake or Milwaukee or St. Louis. Even his Jewish wife, wrapped in the security of multiple generations of American ancestry, didn't worry as he did.

She'd probably already forgotten the incident he still thought of, not infrequently. It had happened a few years earlier, when they'd been visiting Amanda at school and spent an extra day and night in Boston on their own, and as they'd walked down a relatively quiet yet decidedly urban street after dinner, a group of teenagers—teenagers whom he'd instantly imagined must cause nightmares for their parents, tattooed teenagers with heads shaven and clothing ripped—strode up alongside them, their ringleader chanting, "KILL THE KIKES, KILL THE NIGGERS, KILL THE FAGS." And David had seen his wife's head turn toward them in outrage; he knew that in about one second she would open her mouth with the confidence of a woman with bloodlines rooted in the land of the free and the home of the brave, and so he'd yanked her arm—hard, harder maybe than he'd really had to—because what you learned from immigrant-survivor parents like his was that it was better to be quiet, better not to give crazy people any reason to get any crazier. Besides that, you didn't know if these kids were even more dangerous than they appeared. What if they were carrying knives or, God forbid, guns? So in the end all Barbara had said was "Ow!" and by the time she'd absorbed the pain and the shock, as well as the realization that her gentle husband had been the one to inflict them, those teenagers had turned down another street and were out of sight.

"You and your catastrophes," his wife said, starting the climb up the museum's steps. "Go, have a good time."

A few minutes later the bus arrived. More than half the seats were empty; it was easy to take a place by a window and watch the well-kept apartment buildings and the Plaza and the stores pass by until it was time to signal his stop and descend and begin walking west. Each step took him closer to his destination, while he sweated from the sun and his nerves. The hotel would be air-conditioned. It wouldn't smell, as did the streets, of smoke and grease and hot dogs. The sight of big, burly men in blue blazers standing by the main doors and then within the glass-and-metal skyscraper, men adjusting earpieces and talking into tiny microphones, men whose eyes followed him and everyone else stepping onto the escalator to the conference registration floor, pleased and reassured him.

When he reached the front of the G-L line, a kindly conference volunteer found his folder. She heaved a black tote bag bearing the conference name and motto—JEWISH-AMERICAN FAMILY HISTORY CONFERENCE: *DIE GANZE MISHPOCHA*—onto the counter.

"Don't lose your name tag," the conference worker said. "You'll need it to get in to each session." She pushed the tote toward him. He thanked her and moved to an empty table a few feet away. He deposited the bag with a thud and threaded the string they'd given him through the appropriate spaces on the nametag's plastic shield, then placed the item around his neck.

He opened the bag. It was a little overwhelming: the giant red three-ring binder containing the list of attendees and the session descriptions, the presenter biographies and the schedule, the maps and the restaurant recommendations. He dug to the bottom and retrieved a coffee mug evidently provided compliments of Zabar's. That, he'd give to Barbara. She never seemed to have an adequate supply of coffee mugs.

There was so much to do beyond the sessions and seminars he'd already marked on the copy of the schedule he'd printed out back home in his kitchen, so many documentary film screenings to attend and so many booths set up by various museums and libraries in the resource room to visit, and of course so many books and DVDs to examine in the vendors' area that, despite all his planning, he didn't quite know where to begin. Anyway, whatever he chose to do this afternoon would be little more than a way to fill the hours until the special dinner sponsored on this first day of the conference by the Second Generation online discussion group. David's lower left jaw ached as he thought about this dinner. This pain came to him every so often; both Barbara and his dentist insisted that it was stress-related.

But it would be worth the time to review all of this material. First, there was the list of conference registrants, twenty-five pages long. Talk about a diaspora. Just skimming the list, David noted participants hailing from every continent except Antarctica. He thumbed through more. He read a page paying tribute to a genealogist who had recently died. He turned that page quickly, moving on to the hotel fact sheet. Then there was the list of synagogues near the hotel—six of them.

David sighed. He repacked the tote bag. Then he set off to explore as much as he could before dinner.

The dinner, at a restaurant near the hotel, was far better attended than he expected. David arrived a few minutes early and was directed to a private dining room, where he was seated next to a woman named Linda, from Chicago.

Linda waxed enthusiastic about developments in DNA genealogy.

"It's really very simple," she said, as their salad plates were cleared away. "You swab your mouth. You send the saliva sample to the lab. The lab studies the Y chromosome. And a computer compares what they find to the analyses already in their database." Here she paused, as if uncertain that David understood the significance of the Y chromosome, the one his father had given him, and his father's father had given to Max and his brothers, and so on reaching back through generations, for centuries, marking with a genetic stamp all men descended from their common paternal ancestor, whether they were fellow Kaufmanns or, thanks to the vagaries of the Diaspora and the inclinations of immigration officials, Kofmans, Coffmans, or something similar. Apparently, Linda had convinced her brother to participate in her quest to understand their paternal legacy, since her saliva wouldn't do the job.

"I don't know," David said, as grilled salmon was set in front of him. "Are you sure that the labs don't misuse the samples? I mean, they could test for diseases or inherited conditions and then an insurance company—."

"You sound exactly like my brother," Linda said. "So suspicious. I'll tell you what I told him. The reputable places—and you'd only use a reputable place, of course—don't even do that kind of testing. No one outside the lab has access to the samples. And the databases themselves aren't even open to the public."

Before the evening ended, Linda gave him one last sales pitch.

"My father lost everyone," she said. "Or almost everyone. The testing connected us with relatives we didn't know he had. Really distant relatives, sure, but still, relatives."

Even then, David wasn't convinced. But back at the hotel he restructured his carefully set schedule and decided to attend the main DNA presentation, made by a representative from one of the labs, the next morning.

Back home, and after several evenings staring at the computer screen, David ordered a kit from the company the conference presenter had founded (it was the best one out there, David discovered through his post-conference research in genealogy magazines). Tens of thousands of people had already sent their samples to the same lab his would go to. Somehow, somewhere, someone would have to match him. And maybe, then, they could tell him things about his family that his own parents had, whether out of trauma or lack of knowledge, chosen not to share. Or maybe his sample might clue them in to something else entirely; maybe it would link David with the *Cohanim*, the descendants of the biblical Aaron who, he read, numbered significantly among the world's Kaufmanns and their "genetic relatives." Such news his father would surely welcome; beyond added pride in his heritage it would also give Dad something significant to discuss with his new Wynnewood friends.

So it came to pass that one night in early fall—one night, as it happened, between the Holy Days of Rosh Hashanah and Yom Kippur—David Kaufmann stood in his bathroom. He scrubbed his hands with antibacterial soap. He dried them carefully. He opened the kit's plastic bag. With one of the cheek scrapers he swabbed the soft tissue within his mouth ("forcefully," as the directions instructed). Then, his hands so steady it frankly surprised him, he stored the sample in its tube. In the morning he left Barbara still asleep in their bed and he repeated the procedure with the second scraper and tube that were marked with his kit number. He signed the release forms and mailed everything back to the laboratory. Then he waited. And waited. He'd ordered the most expensive and elaborate test—the Y-DNA 67, which would test his sample for sixty-seven markers for genetic matches with other males in the database. He'd have to wait a while.

Eight weeks later—checking his e-mail in the kitchen before breakfast—he had the results.

He didn't tell Barbara immediately. For an entire day he went about his business. Literally. He drove to his office. He answered inquiries from clients. He conducted a staff meeting and mediated a quarrel between two of his partners. At lunchtime he ate a tuna sandwich at his desk, and then he simply kept working, kept going, five hours more before driving home, listening intently to public radio as he drove. Even once he'd parked the car in the driveway, unlocked and de-alarmed the house and begun mixing the evening's salad, he still managed not to think about it, and that wasn't easy because right there in the kitchen, humming away as usual on the table in the corner, was the source of his discovery. The electronic Tree of Knowledge.

Only after he had cleared the dinner plates and Barbara was placing them in the dishwasher did he return to the computer and print everything out; only after he'd reread the company's explanations of everything from the language ("alleles" and "markers") to how they calculated common ancestor estimates; only once he'd heard Barbara shut the faucet for the last time and issue her usual sigh before turning away to leave the room did he clear his throat and call for her and hand her the pages.

"Wait," she said. "I need my glasses."

Then, a few minutes later: "So what does it mean?"

He told her. He explained that while his DNA sample had not matched with any of the Kaufmann (or Kaufman, Kofman, or Coffman) men in the database—and there were many, another reason why he'd selected this particular company to run his test—it had matched 67 potential markers out of 67 with five other men in the database. Who all shared a surname.

McMahon. Or MacMahon.

"That means," he said, "that my—father—belongs to the same group."

"So your father has another surname?"

He didn't answer.

"My God. Your father is named *McMahon*?"

He still couldn't answer.

Barbara thought for a moment. "Do you think Max's mother—?" Her eyebrows arched. "Do you think your grandmother had an affair?"

That got him speaking. "No, I don't. I mean, I don't know anything about her, but I seriously doubt she had an affair. Let alone with a man named McMahon. Somehow I don't think there were too many McMahons running around Germany eighty-something years ago, do you?"

Barbara paused. "Well, then," she said. "Well, then. Is it possible that—your father isn't really your father?"

David just looked at her.

"I mean," she went on. "You always felt Esther was

keeping things from you. I'm not saying she had an affair, necessarily." She paused. "Maybe—she was—I know, it's horrible to even think about. But it would make sense, if she didn't ever want to revisit that, or tell you about it."

"Stop it!" Like a child he covered his ears.

She looked again at the printouts. "It says here," she began. "It says here that they're willing to run the test again if you think there may be a lab error. They'll even try to speed it up. If it turns out that they made a mistake, they won't charge for the retest."

He bit his lip before he responded. "And what if they haven't made a mistake?"

"Well," Barbara said. "Then you're out fifty dollars." She paused. "But wouldn't that be the least of it?"

They ran the test again. In the meantime, life went on. David went to work, went home, went to the dentist because the jaw pain was so much worse.

And on Sundays, David went to visit his father. That was the hardest part.

On Sundays, typically, Barbara caught up with her personal e-mails (and grumbled over the ones from students who seemed to expect her to be accessible 24/7) and phone calls and stole some time to read whatever novel her book group had chosen while David sealed and strapped himself into his car and drove to Wynnewood. Every Sunday David parked the car in the lot, and walked through the extra-wide front doors, and smiled at whichever receptionist and guard sat on duty at the desk. He complimented the nice fresh flowers standing in the vase beside the guest registry as he accepted the pen that was offered. In one column he printed his name, DAVID KAUFMANN, and in the next column, the name of the resident he was there to see, MAX KAUFMANN, and the time, which was usually, but not always, between 2 and 2:30 p.m.

This routine David followed while he waited for those second test results, too. But it wasn't easy sitting in his father's room. Looking at his father, and not knowing what he should be thinking. Talking—about Wynnewood, about work, about Barbara, about Jon in Jerusalem and Amanda and her new boyfriend, about the latest errant politician in the news—as if everything were normal. Although everything still might be absolutely that. Normal.

"David, my son, you look upset," his father said as David prepared to leave him on the last of those intervening Sundays. "Is something wrong?"

"No, Dad. Just tired."

Then the second results came back. Again he printed them out and handed them to his wife.

"Looks like I've just lost fifty dollars," he said.

These results arrived on a Friday. Sunday he'd again be expected at Wynnewood.

Somehow, even this day, the day he'd prepared to leave his house with the printouts jammed within his jacket pocket, even as his heart raced and his head pounded and he finished loading the lunchtime plates and glasses into the dishwasher and closed that machine with a faster-and-louder-than-usual *thwunk* and as Barbara looked up from her book and her coffee (in the Zabar's mug, as it happened), frowning, and offered once again to accompany him, he still managed to drive and to park, to walk and to compliment and to sign his name.

"Your dad'll be waiting for you in his room," the receptionist said. "Like always."

David nodded, a smile forcing itself across his face. "Thanks."

His father's walker was parked outside the door. David knocked, quickly.

"It's open," his father called.

David paused. He waited a few seconds and breathed deeply. Only then did he open the door.

"Hi, Dad," he said, and as the old man began to brace himself against the chair he added, "No, don't get up." Of course, had his father risen David would once again have had the opportunity to remark on the noticeable difference between their heights. Once, David had commented on this; his mother had murmured, so softly that David had had to lean closer to hear her, that her own father had been a tall man, too.

But now Max remained seated; David leaned down and kissed his cheek. Covered with a blue and yellow afghan David's mother had knitted long ago, Max rested in one of the two heavy, upholstered-in-brown armchairs they'd moved here from the apartment. David moved to the other one. He leaned back against the pillow with the bright floral needlepoint cover his mother had also sewn, uncountable years back.

"Good weekend?" he asked his father.

"David, my son," his father began, in the accented voice David knew so well, the voice that had read newspaper articles aloud at so many mealtimes and had sung him so many "Happy Birthday"s and had led all the guests in chanting the prayers over the bread and the wine at David and Barbara's wedding and at their son's *bris* and at the kids' Bar and Bat Mitzvah celebrations. "Every weekend we are alive is a good weekend, and it's especially good now that you are here."

For more than fifty years—as long as David had known him—his father had insisted that every day was a good day, every weekend a good weekend. Even when David, as a child, had heard him shout out in the night. Even when his father's eyes clouded over that day David had first asked about the numbers on his arm. Even, in fact, when David's mother had died. His father had shown himself far more composed on that occasion than David had managed to be. After the funeral Max had stood there, sadly but steadily, on the soil by her grave and said, "And how many men can spend their lives with such a woman? What is there to be sad about, really?"

In a way, it was amazing. And in a way, it was not surprising at all. Because compared to what Max Kaufmann had endured in the five years before he met his wife at the DP camp, or what David had come to guess he had endured, everything else must seem a proverbial picnic.

David's jaw ached. He gritted his teeth, then took another breath.

"There's something I need to discuss with you," he said.

When David had finished speaking, they were both silent.

"So, Dad," David said, then. "Do you understand everything I've said so far?"

His father nodded. David waited. Maybe if he waited his father would just come out with the explanation he was waiting for.

But all his father said was, "Can you help me to the

bathroom?"

David helped him stand and supported him, lightly, as they crossed the room. Once inside, his father could manage on his own.

"Can you explain it?" he finally asked, after they'd resettled in the chairs.

And now, behind their glasses, his father's eyes shone. For a quick moment the old man glanced over to the photographs of David and Barbara and their children. In his face David saw all the pain of the cries in the night, the question about the numbers, the loss of his wife. Magnified.

"Yes, David," his father said at last, softly. "I can."

The story began, his father told him, at David's childhood home, the building at the corner of York Avenue and East 88th Street. It was set above a bakery, and each morning Max and Esther awakened to the pleasing scents of baking breads and sweet rolls. "You can't imagine what that meant to us," said his father. "We'd spent so much time hungry, each of us, and for so long we'd smelled things—not so beautiful."

Neither of them slept particularly well (here his father cleared his throat, maybe remembering the shouts that had wakened and worried David), but before the clock rang every morning, before Max reached for his spectacles, before Esther opened her eyes, they smelled those breads, baking. They lived on the second floor. There were six apartments on each of the five floors, and they were pleased to be exactly where they were; the building had no elevator and carrying groceries and laundry up so many flights of stairs would have been too much, still. Especially for Esther.

They had many sources for sorrow, his father admitted. But the one that was new, the one they'd not known Over There, but discovered instead Right Here, was the news that Esther could not bear children. This was something she'd suspected might be true—it had been foolish, maybe, to even hope that after everything her body had endured Over There it would be able to bring forth healthy life. But she needed to hear this conclusion not once, not twice, but three times, in three different doctors' voices, to believe it.

Of course, this saddened them. As bad as they knew the world could be, as much as they knew of the human capacity to do evil, they hadn't given up. They hadn't given up on their own survival and now, especially Over Here, where they seemed slowly to be moving ahead, into the future, they'd have been willing to take a risk, to produce something tiny and vulnerable that would be their responsibility to nurture and care for. In their minds they'd each imagined children named for all the Lost, their own beloved parents, especially. They'd imagined taking up once again the chain of life that the

Nazis had worked so diligently to break.

"But," said his father, "It wasn't to be." And after a few solitary crying jags—hers in the apartment, his at his desk—they stored this sadness away, too.

David brought his father a glass of water, and Max continued speaking.

One spring morning in 1952 he'd left the apartment for work. He had closed the door and turned around to see a woman stepping out from the adjacent apartment. She was tall, almost his height. She wore a dark blue suit with matching shoes. Gloves. She was so strikingly beautiful—"a face like you might see on a poster or a signboard"—that he almost stared.

"Hello," she'd said, shyly.

"Hello." He hadn't realized new tenants had settled in next door.

"I just moved in," she said. Her voice was American, but different from the American voices he heard every day.

He nodded. "Nice to meet you."

"Heading out to work?" she asked.

He nodded again.

"Me, too."

A working woman. Did she have a husband? Children? What kind of work did she do? Where? It wasn't polite to ask, it wasn't any of his business.

"I saw you yesterday," she said. "You and your wife? You must have been returning from somewhere. I saw you from the window."

"Ah," he said.

They reached the front door. He held it open. She descended the steps to the sidewalk, and turned left. He turned right.

"She met Esther soon after that," Max said, refocusing his eyes on David. "I don't remember how much after that. Perhaps it was the next day. Or the next week."

And apparently Esther had discovered much more about the new neighbor—including her name, which was Bridget—than Max had. She'd learned, for example, that Bridget had been staying with a girlfriend for her first few months in New York. But now she had a job—a job as a secretary, in a publishing house. So she'd found her own apartment.

"They got along very well," his father recalled. Esther seemed to like the young woman. She was a lively girl, with plenty of stories to tell. Esther liked to listen; apparently, Bridget liked to be heard.

Esther's interest in their neighbor—the conversations whose soft buzz he could still hear even when he'd retreated into the bedroom and the two women sat talking at the table, and the bursts of laughter that might punctuate them—pleased him. For he loved his wife. And, especially after the third doctor's declaration, he had not often heard her laugh.

The two women seemed to spend so much time to-gether—and yet who was he to judge such things?—that it was hardly a surprise one evening when Esther reported, "I saw Bridget today."

"Yes?" he'd replied.

"She's in trouble," Esther said.

"What's the matter?"

"She's in *trouble*," Esther repeated, meaningfully, and when Max remained uncomprehending added, "She—is going to have a child."

"She tells you this?" he asked.

Esther shrugged. "She needed to tell someone."

They had entered the building, the women, at the same time that afternoon. Bridget's eyes were red and her lips were pale.

"Something is wrong?" Esther had asked. They'd spent the next two hours sitting there in the apartment (quite possibly in these very chairs, David realized as he listened) while Esther made tea and poured it and Bridget wept and choked out her story.

The child's father—Bridget's employer—had money. A lot of money. He was an important person, this Mr. McMahon. He was willing to send Bridget somewhere to "have the matter attended to," as Bridget had told Esther. But he already had a wife. He already had children.

Here Max had recoiled, just a bit. "Did she know this, about this man, that he was married, when she—?"

Esther stared at him. "And that matters why?"

"Well," he said, and then said nothing else.

And what of Bridget's own family?

"Can you imagine, a Catholic girl? She's terrified of her parents, her priest, all of them." Thus had Esther, with a few words and a wave of her hand, dismissed their potential assistance.

"Where is she from, again? Ohio, is it?"

"Indiana," Esther said. "Her father teaches at that big Catholic university there."

Neither of them said it. That maybe this was part of God's plan. That maybe, He would give them a child this way, and help the child's mother (who'd shuddered as she'd confided to Esther what McMahon wanted her to do, now, a mortal sin to compound everything else they'd done; she couldn't imagine not having this baby, and yet she knew she couldn't raise it herself).

And at the same time there'd be added to the world one more Jewish soul, from which still others might be created (here, as David listened, the images of his own son and daughter came to him; they appeared first as babies, and then as the adults they'd become, and then his eyes moved to their photographs in his father's room) to recover all those that had been lost.

They'd used the man's money, his father explained, to move Bridget to a building on the West Side. There she waited out the pregnancy. After it was all over she'd go home to Indiana. Start over. Of course she didn't return to work, and Mr. McMahon didn't exactly go searching for her.

They'd agreed to this move to another apartment—Bridget and Esther and Max—because this way, none of their other neighbors would be the wiser. As Bridget's pregnancy progressed Esther strapped a cushion—a seam of which she repeatedly tore open so that more padding could be stuffed within it—to her own middle. "When is the baby due?" others asked Esther as her "pregnancy" advanced. "Late April," she'd answer, smiling.

The baby had indeed arrived in late April. Esther stayed in Bridget's apartment for the duration of the confinement, again so as not to arouse any neighbors' suspicions. Each day Esther and Max went to the hospital to see the baby boy. They finalized the arrangements. Thus, their return home with the baby a week later—the day of the *bris*, "a joyous day for me, the day I named my beloved son for my father," Max concluded, a few tears escaping his eyes—seemed to their neighbors the most natural thing in the world.

By the time the story was finished it was after 6 p.m.,

well beyond the time that Max—exhausted—should have left his room for the evening meal in the Wynnewood dining hall.

David's BlackBerry buzzed. It had to be Barbara. Probably even she was starting to worry.

What was the correct thing to say now? David didn't know. He simply didn't know. So what he said, in a very gentle voice as he passed his father a tissue, was this: "Thank you for telling me, Dad." There would be other visits, other Sundays, when they could talk more.

He accompanied the old man to the dining hall and, impulsively, kissed him. More tears ran down the fissures on Max's face. "Dad, really. It's all right. I'll see you next week. And I'll call you tomorrow," David said, and heard his own words echo as he left the building, returned to the car and drove home.

Was it really "all right"? Even after talking it all over with Barbara; even after scheduling a time for Amanda to come home and for Jon to be on speakerphone and be told ("I thought you had cancer!" Amanda had cried, relieved, when he'd revealed the reason for these arrangements); even after he'd made a month's-worth more visits to Wynnewood, he still didn't know what it meant to have this information.

What he knew was that he'd learned something revelatory. He'd have to rethink so much. He certainly wasn't about to instantly shelve all his ideas about himself and his heritage ("Does this mean we're half-Catholic?" Jon had asked, from Jerusalem, and David had been stunned by the vehemence of his reply: "We're Jews!"). And he was hardly about to dispense with—or ever, ever forget—all the research he'd done.

But he couldn't ignore it. Not now. Now he faced other quests, other names, other people. There'd be other discussion groups and lists. There'd almost certainly be a trip to Indiana.

When he was ready—just before his birthday—he sat again at the kitchen computer. He e-mailed the host of the McMahon surname group. He gave a short history. Then he wrote: "I have a 67/67 match with at least five of your group's members. May I join?"

Made in the USA
Charleston, SC
20 April 2011